Cross-Dressing Villainess Cecilia Sylvie

Hiroro Akizakura

Illustration by **Dangmill**

Cross-Dressing Villainess Cecilia Sylvie 1

Hiroro Akizakura

TRANSLATION BY SARAH TANGNEY ❁ COVER ART BY DANGMILL

This book is a work of fiction. Names, characters, places, and incidents are the product of the author's imagination or are used fictitiously. Any resemblance to actual events, locales, or persons, living or dead, is coincidental.

AKUYAKU REIJO, CECILIA SYLVIE WA SHINITAKUNAI
NODE DANSO SURUKOTO NI SHITA. Vol.1
©Hiroro Akizakura 2019
First published in Japan in 2019 by KADOKAWA CORPORATION, Tokyo.
English translation rights arranged with KADOKAWA CORPORATION, Tokyo,
through TUTTLE-MORI AGENCY, INC., Tokyo.

English translation © 2022 by Yen Press, LLC

Yen Press, LLC supports the right to free expression and the value of copyright. The purpose of copyright is to encourage writers and artists to produce the creative works that enrich our culture.

The scanning, uploading, and distribution of this book without permission is a theft of the author's intellectual property. If you would like permission to use material from the book (other than for review purposes), please contact the publisher. Thank you for your support of the author's rights.

Yen On
150 West 30th Street, 19th Floor
New York, NY 10001

Visit us at yenpress.com • facebook.com/yenpress • twitter.com/yenpress
yenpress.tumblr.com • instagram.com/yenpress

First Yen On Edition: January 2022

Yen On is an imprint of Yen Press, LLC.
The Yen On name and logo are trademarks of Yen Press, LLC.

The publisher is not responsible for websites (or their content) that are not owned by the publisher.

Library of Congress Cataloging-in-Publication Data
Names: Akizakura, Hiroro, author. | Dangmill, illustrator. | Tangney, Sarah, translator.
Title: Cross-dressing villainess Cecilia Sylvie / Hiroro Akizakura ; illustration by Dangmill ; translation by Sarah Tangney.
Other titles: Akuyaku reijo, cecilia sylvie wa shinitakunai. English
Description: First Yen On edition. | New York, NY : Yen On, 2021. | Audience: Ages 13+ |
Summary: Reincarnated as a villainess in a video game, Cecilia avoids her death flag by masquerading as a man, crossdressing and assuming a new identity, trying not to let her guise slip with the prince.
Identifiers: LCCN 2021039071 | ISBN 9781975334215 (v. 1 ; trade paperback) |
ISBN 9781975334239 (v. 2 ; trade paperback)
Subjects: CYAC: Fantasy. | Male impersonators—Fiction. | Video games—Fiction. |
Secrets—Fiction. | Princes—Fiction. | LCGFT: Fantasy fiction. | Light novels.
Classification: LCC PZ7.1.A3927 Cr 2021 | DDC [Fic]—dc23
LC record available at https://lccn.loc.gov/2021039071

ISBNs: 978-1-9753-3421-5 (paperback)
978-1-9753-3422-2 (ebook)

1 3 5 7 9 10 8 6 4 2

LSC-C

Printed in the United States of America

CONTENTS

Name: Cecilia Sylvie

Gilbert Sylvie
Cecilia's younger adoptive brother and a love interest in the game. Helps her dress as a boy at school.
Oscar Abel Prosper
Crown prince. Cecilia's fiancé and a love interest in the game.
Cecilia Sylvie
Daughter of Duke Sylvie. A villainess who appears in Holy Maiden of Vleugel Academy 3.
Cecil Admina
Cecilia's male alter ego and the son of a baron. Known as the school prince.

Character Introductions

Jade Benjamin

A young businessman and a potential love interest. Seems to have something going on with Lean.

Lean Rhazaloa

Daughter of a baron. The protagonist of Holy Maiden of Vleugel Academy 3.

Cross-Dressing Villainess Cecilia Sylvie

Dante Hampton

Oscar's friend who is also romanceable in Holy Maiden of Vleugel Academy 3. Has a secret he can't tell anyone...

✦ Prologue ✦

Dearest Mama and Papa,

Please forgive me for not being your ideal daughter.
In order to live a peaceful and carefree life from now on, I, Cecilia Sylvie…

…have decided to become a boy!

Cecilia Sylvie, daughter of a duke, was only five years old when she realized something that could rock the very foundations of this world, something that revealed it for what it really was.

So earth-shattering was this revelation that she didn't dare say a peep about it, even at the age of five, fearing that it would cause her anxious mother and maid to turn pale and call for doctors if she let it slip. Still, she couldn't just pretend like all was well in the face of the twisted shape of her world and her own bleak future. Subsequently, she came down with a fever and was laid up in bed for a week.

Namely, the truth Cecilia realized was that she had transmigrated into the world of the girl's dating sim *Holy Maiden of Vleugel Academy 3*.

And Cecilia Sylvie was the main character's love rival. In other words, she was the villainess of the story.

Even before this realization, she'd always felt that something had been off.

She would sometimes get the distinct sensation that she had someone else's memories mixed in with hers; she would meet someone for the first time and already know them somehow or would envision unimaginable foods she'd never eaten before, such as "instant ramen." That last one almost tasted so real it made her mouth water.

Thanks to all this, her parents thought of her as a little bit special, but they loved her all the same. In fact, they spoiled their one and only daughter rotten. They bought her anything she wanted, instructed the servants and maids to prioritize her above all else, and anticipated her every whim.

In short, they were overly indulgent parents who had raised a spoiled, irresponsible, and selfish daughter.

And in fairness, up until that moment, Cecilia had indeed been an *incredibly* selfish girl.

Happily thinking of herself as the center of the universe, she spent money with such flagrancy that it was clear she didn't understand the concept of wastefulness. She believed she could get absolutely anything she wanted if she only cried hard enough, and she was entirely convinced that she had a bright future in store.

But upon meeting *him*, her entire personality changed.

Gilbert Coulson, presently known as Gilbert Sylvie.

The Coulsons were distant relatives, and he was adopted into Cecilia's family as her brother, one year younger than her.

The instant she laid eyes on him, she froze as though she'd been struck with a powerful bolt of lightning.

That was because she knew him.

Gilbert Sylvie was a love interest in *Holy Maiden of Vleugel Academy 3*.

There, he had been moody, submissive, and preferred to stay shut up in his room, perhaps because Cecilia treated him as her servant, heedless of the fact that Gilbert had become the son and heir of House Sylvie.

While his age, overall look, and expressions did not match up with her memories of the character, his hair, as black as a wet raven's wings, and eyes of obsidian were unmistakable.

And then memories of her previous life flooded in one after another…

But there, Cecilia changed her mind, reminding herself that there was no way that was possible.

Which was understandable. Ordinarily, no one would have believed her. Yet, those undeniable memories of her past life brought a swift end to her selfish behavior.

The month after Gilbert came to live with the Sylvies, her distinct sense of unease was wholly validated. It happened when she first made her high society debut, accompanied by her father.

There, she met another love interest from the game…

Oscar Abel Prosper.

The son of the king of Prosper. In other words, the crown prince and the man who was set to become Cecilia's fiancé in two years.

The moment she learned the identity of this arrogant redhead, she collapsed, frothing at the mouth.

As for why, there was the fact that she'd witnessed with her own eyes that the unreal was actually very real. But there was also her despair for her own fate—which was probably the most accurate explanation.

None of the endings for Cecilia Sylvie in *Holy Maiden of Vleugel Academy 3* were happy ones.

The only lots that awaited her were a painful death or a quick death.

The second she realized she might die at seventeen, she made a grand decision to stave off her looming fate twelve years hence.

"Okay, then. I'll become a boy!"

Yes, Cecilia Sylvie decided to dress as a boy to avoid her tragic fate.

✦ CHAPTER 1 ✦ Selection Ceremony

Vleugel Academy had its very own prince.

He had hair of translucent gold and eyes of sapphire blue.

He was long-limbed, with an androgynous face that could charm anyone.

He glided silently through the halls with all the grace of a single white rose.

If a girl tripped in front of him, he would smoothly offer her a hand and whisper to her in his mellifluous voice with his beautiful features, "Are you hurt in any way, my princess?"

That was when squeals of joy would rise up from out of nowhere.

The prince was named Cecil Admina.

The alter ego of one Cecilia Sylvie, the seventeen-year-old daughter of a duke.

"Mmm, why did things end up like this...?" Cecil, or rather Cecilia, grumbled as she gazed up at the glazed glass roof of the academy greenhouse. Next to her on the bench sat her sixteen-year-old younger brother, Gilbert.

They were the only two people in the standalone greenhouse, which was her one and only haven in the school, the only place where girls would not call out, "My prince!" and pursue Cecil.

"I just wanted to blend in and keep to myself here, so why have I become the school prince…?" She sighed.

"That's because you're a nitwit, Sister," answered Gilbert.

"Guh!"

His words cut like a dagger to the heart.

Gilbert was supposed to have grown up to be dour and moody under Cecilia's heel, but now—twelve years after they'd first met—he'd transformed into a sharp-tongued, sassy little thing. That was more or less to be expected since she hadn't bullied him like in the game, but still, she wished he'd grown up to be a little bit cuter…

Undaunted by his sister's glare, Gilbert threw her an exasperated look. "What was that '*Are you hurt in any way, my princess?*' nonsense from this morning, then? You sure seem to spout the most cringeworthy lines as if they were nothing."

"Hey, I can't have anyone noticing that I'm really a girl. Obviously, I have to act even manlier than a normal guy!" she protested.

"That's your idea of manly?"

"If you want to know the most popular type of character in the dating sims I played for eighteen years of my last life, then yes, that's it!"

"…Yeah, which is what caused all this," Gilbert deadpanned once again.

In Cecilia's past life, she'd been Hiyono Kanzaki, a high schooler who'd been a major fan of dating sims featuring casts of handsome men.

Hiyono was the type to blow almost all her allowance on dating sims, and if she didn't have enough money to snap everything up at once, she would work a part-time job to cover the rest. Staying up all night gaming until dawn broke the dark night sky was an everyday occurrence, and she often spent weekends holed up in her room.

She'd been a member of the theater club at school and had put her all into it with her fellow club members, and she'd liked fashion, too. But dating sims were far and away her favorite hobby.

Holy Maiden of Vleugel Academy 3 was one of the games Hiyono had played back then.

"So you're telling me you were really chosen to be the Holy Maiden?" Gilbert went on. "I mean, yeah, the current one's been there a long time, and I heard her powers are starting to wane. But for *you* to get chosen as the representative of the most squeaky-clean and pure of maidens, I almost wonder if the world's gone mad..."

"Wait, Gil, do you hate me?"

"Not at all, I love you. I just think that someone as rough and careless as you wouldn't really be able to fulfill the position's duties."

"You're so mean to me!" she squawked indignantly.

As Gilbert broke into a grin, Cecilia buried her face in her hands.

As the title implied, *Holy Maiden of Vleugel Academy 3* was the third game in the *Holy Maiden of Vleugel Academy* series.

In this world, there is a Holy Maiden who protects and guides the people. Even the king cannot disregard what she says.

The protagonist, Lean Rhazaloa, raised as a commoner, and the villainess, Cecilia Sylvie, become candidates to receive the title of Holy Maiden and compete with each other at Vleugel Academy. That's the gist of the narrative.

"I didn't want to get picked, either..."

"Why do you sound like it's already too late?"

"The night before last, a rose-shaped mark appeared around my chest...," she revealed.

Picking up on what she was implying, Gilbert's face froze as he murmured, "Oh..."

A special feature would manifest on the bodies of potential Holy Maidens to signify their candidacy—the mark of the rose, in Cecilia's case.

In the game, the story begins when Lean discovers a snowflake-shaped mark on the back of her hand. The following day at her new school, Vleugel Academy, she learns that she has been selected as a Holy Maiden candidate.

Today was probably when Lean would transfer in. It takes place a week after the senior students' entrance ceremony in the dating sim. That meant her mark must have appeared on her hand the night before.

"So I guess it's a done deal, then. You're a potential Holy Maiden," Gilbert noted.

"Exactly! And I need you to back me up! You're seriously the only one I can rely on! Help give your big sister a bright and peaceful future!"

"Yeah, fine, I got it! Hey, don't start hugging me!" he yelped, pushing her away by the head as she attempted to launch herself at him the way she had when they were younger. A flush formed on his cheeks, likely out of embarrassment.

Cecilia, the villain to the protagonist, meets a tragic end. She dies in every single route—the normal route, the romantic endings, and the bad ending. It doesn't matter. All that changes is the way she expires.

Thus, Cecilia had decided to become a boy. Not only were they fundamentally unable to become Holy Maidens, but as a male student, she could also fade into the scenery as an unremarkable background character. That being said, she didn't actually plan to live as a man from here on out. It was just about blending in at the elite boarding school that served as the setting of the game…

But there were limits to what she could accomplish alone.

She'd pulled some strings at the academy ahead of time,

pretended to fall ill to get out of appearing at social events, helped her father with his work to save up some money for emergencies, practiced binding her unnecessarily large breasts quickly, secretly constructed a wig out of her own hair…

Although she'd spent the twelve years since getting her memories back making all those preparations, she still could neither obtain a male academy uniform in an inconspicuous way, nor could she arrange for a false identity as a baron's son.

For that, she'd roped in her younger brother, Gilbert, for help.

He hadn't laughed at his sister for talking about her past life or games. Instead, he'd simply replied, "So what do you need me to do, then?"

For that, she couldn't thank him enough. Despite his mouthy attitude, he truly did love his sister.

Pushing away from Cecilia's grip, he cleared his throat and trained his face into a composed expression. "Anyway, isn't today when Lean transfers into your class? Shouldn't you get back to your classroom? You don't want to show up late and attract attention."

"Oh yeah. Yeah, you're right. But soon…"

The instant she said that and met his gaze, however, an announcement came over the speakers installed throughout the school. It instructed that all students go to the auditorium for an urgent assembly.

For an academy that had such a strictly regimented schedule, it was exceedingly rare for a school-wide assembly to be called via announcement. Typically, they would have been given some sort of notice a day beforehand.

"Does that mean it's started?"

"Yeah. Probably," she answered, her face tight.

He patted her shoulder encouragingly. "Well, let's go. No use hiding out."

"True," she replied.

They got up from the bench and exited the greenhouse.

Someone was watching them from behind.

"Hee-hee-hee. I found Gilbert," said the person in a cutesy voice, her intense gaze glued to the two of them as they walked away.

With her pale lips curved upward in glee, she clutched a thick notebook and pen in her hands.

"Ah, at last, this day has come. I've been waiting so, so long for this," she babbled with rapturous delight, hugging herself. Her cheeks glowed pink, and her eyes glistened with tears, probably from excitement more than anything else.

She had slightly wavy pink hair and long eyelashes framing big, ruby eyes. Though she wore no lipstick, her small lips boasted a natural tinge of red, and her dainty physique stoked a natural desire in men to protect her.

Her name was Lean Rhazaloa, daughter of a baron.

The heroine of *Holy Maiden of Vleugel Academy 3.*

"You have all been brought here today for no other purpose than the selection of a new Holy Maiden. The Sphere of Stars chooses the candidates for both the knights and the next Holy Maiden simultaneously..."

From the auditorium stage, a religious clergyman of some sort, dispatched by the crown, droned on and on. Accompanied by sweeping gesticulations, his speech dragged on for so long that the students were stifling yawns.

In fact, the prologue to this game is so excessive in length that Cecilia's past identity, Hiyono, had saved the game right before the first chapter so she could start from that point for every subsequent playthrough. She'd only ever gotten all the way through the prologue once.

But why is it so long in the first place? And this guy goes on forever, too, but I feel like there's some sort of other reason for it...

As she pondered the situation, the man continued to blather away.

To sum up his long-winded, roundabout address: The Sphere of Stars had heralded the appearance of the potential Holy Maidens, so the Selection Ceremony for the title would commence.

There were three candidates, and the divine revelation indicated that all were academy students.

Accordingly, the Selection Ceremony would take place at Vleugel Academy.

Additionally, the seven knights who would protect the Holy Maiden would now be chosen.

That was all.

Incidentally, the Holy Maiden needed this Sphere of Stars to receive oracles, and the seven knights were the game's love interests.

Chosen by Sacred Artifacts, the seven knights would pick the most fitting Holy Maiden and gift her their Artifact over the course of the year. The candidate with the greatest number of Artifacts would become the next Holy Maiden.

Hence, the year leading up to the appointment of the new Holy Maiden was known as the Selection Ceremony.

The Selection Ceremony is essentially an election, thought Cecilia, gazing up at the man who was *still* prattling on from the stage.

By design, the Selection Ceremony required the potential Holy Maidens to win the affections of the knights and at least one more Sacred Artifact than their opponents. Then the Holy Maiden Elect would bestow upon one of the knights who had bequeathed her his Sacred Artifact the title of Holy Knight, which granted him the right to remain by the Holy Maiden's side forever after. That is to say, he assumed the role of her boyfriend.

If I don't come forward as a potential Holy Maiden, the Sacred Artifacts will go to Lean by default, and then I'll be free! At the very least, even if Lean doesn't get a single one, I'll have zero anyway, so it won't matter to me!

The knights have the right to give their candidate their Sacred Artifact, but they also have the right to keep it. If they don't think anyone would be a fitting Holy Maiden, they don't have to hand their Artifact over.

In the event that things end in a tie because no one gives away their Artifacts, the game is set up so that Lean's protagonist status and privilege make her the next Holy Maiden anyway. Regardless, Cecilia would die the same as always in this scenario, but only if she were still a candidate for Holy Maiden. As Cecil, a powerless background character, she should be able to avoid that terrible fate.

If I can make it past this, I'll be safe! All I have to do is keep quiet and support Lean's love life!

While Cecilia was engaging in simplistic daydreams, another man came up behind the clergyman. A white cloth covered both his hands, upon which sat seven glittering silver bracelets. These were the Sacred Artifacts. The seven men they chose were—

The crown prince: Oscar Abel Prosper
Cecilia's younger adoptive brother: Gilbert Sylvie
The young entrepreneur: Jade Benjamin
The mysterious doctor: Mordred Nelson
Oscar's good friend: Dante Hampton
Similar but not identical twins: Eins Machias and Zwei Machias

Within these bracelets dwell spirits that served the gods, and according to legend, the knights are chosen based on their affinities with those spirits. The Artifacts are the manifestations of each knight's talents.

When a knight takes off his Sacred Artifact and slides it onto the wrist of his chosen Holy Maiden, that counts as a vote for her. A single candidate can wear up to seven.

When the man lifted the cloth up to the heavens, the bracelets gave off a faint shimmer. The knights would now be chosen.

Just as the Artifacts rose into the air and scattered in seven directions…

"AAAAAAAHHHHHH!"

…a piercing scream echoed throughout the auditorium.

Cecilia turned around to see a male student pinning a girl to the floor. He was strangling the life out of her astride her prone form. As his fingers pressed deeply against her carotid artery, she writhed in pain.

"Oh no, it's an—"

Cecilia sucked in a breath at the sight of the black miasma emanating from the boy.

Holy Maiden of Vleugel Academy 3 contains RPG battle elements not usually found in dating sims. The characters all have levels.

The enemies are called Obstructions, a sort of monster that clings to the negative emotions of humans and animals. The Obstructions themselves are not all that strong, but they can cause harm to people by boosting their hosts' abilities and throwing their emotions into disarray. These monsters lurk all throughout the country, and under normal circumstances, the Holy Maiden is responsible for vanquishing them. But with the current Holy Maiden's powers weakening, they start to pop up all over. These events are part of the game's backstory.

And the number one sign that an Obstruction had possessed someone or something was black miasma rising from their body.

This boy was undoubtedly under the control of an Obstruction.

"Ah, aaah, ahhh…," moaned the girl, starting to convulse.

"If someone doesn't do something, she's going to—," muttered

Cecilia, looking around to see if anyone was going to help, but the boy's transformation had left them frozen in place.

True, anyone would be petrified to suddenly behold this sight. If she didn't have memories from her past life, Cecilia would have been the same way. But since she did have them, she could process the situation immediately.

Cecilia was the only person capable of acting under these circumstances. She knew that an Obstruction had possessed the student.

Breaking into a run, she hurled herself against him. The momentum sent her rolling into a wall, slamming against it and knocking all the air out of her lungs. Tears pricked her eyes.

The boy she'd rammed into had fallen but then staggered to his feet and stared down at her with unfocused eyes.

Oh, crap! Is this what they look like in real life?! This is straight-up terrifying!

Controlling a character from the game screen, as it turns out, was *nothing* like actually going up against an enemy in person. She managed stand back up, but her legs were still unsteady as her opponent glared at her.

I—I think the way to win is...

Memories of her past life flashed through her mind.

Defeating it with a Sacred Artifact? ...Oh, a potential Holy Maiden or knight needs to touch the mark that's somewhere on the Obstruction!

Then the boy launched himself at Cecilia. As she narrowly dodged him, she watched him carefully.

Now all the effort she'd put in to get fit and strong over the last twelve years—anticipating that something like this might happen—was paying off. And, well, that was why her brother had denounced her as rough and wild, but hey, since her training was coming in handy, that didn't matter now.

Shaking off the boy's grasp, she aimed a kick at his solar plexus. But instead of losing consciousness, the crazed student only grabbed the leg she'd shot at his belly.

"Legendary Hans Kick!"

While shouting an unspeakably lame attack name, Cecilia twisted her leg in his grasp and kicked up at the side of his head. Despite its awful title, the technique was effective, and the boy slid back down to the floor.

She'd found her groove, and her legs were no longer wobbling.

"There it is!" she cried, catching sight of a black mark that resembled ivy on the student's left wrist and leaping at him, heedless of potential injury to herself. It was obvious that things would only get worse if the fight dragged on. The Obstruction provided him with an inexhaustible supply of strength.

Though he was thrashing around violently, he calmed down the instant Cecilia touched his wrist. As the black mist hissed out of him, he went limp and crumpled to the ground.

Cecilia fell on top of him.

"Sis— Uh, Cecil! Are you okay?!" shouted Gilbert. The first to come running up to her was indeed her precious little brother. As he helped her up, she screwed her face up into a grimace. "M-man, that was sooooo scary..."

"Then why did you throw yourself into the fray like that?"

"I mean, the person he was attacking was in danger. My body just moved on its own..."

"Still..."

Only then did she realize that it was dead quiet. Looking around, she saw that all eyes were on her. The boy, Cecilia, and Gilbert, who had come to help her up, were the only ones in the middle of a circle of people.

Scanning the crowd once more, she noticed Lean in the front. She was frozen stiff and staring at Cecilia.

Oh no... This can't be...

The second it hit her, a cold shiver ran up her spine.

This is the tutorial battle!

Explanation time! A tutorial battle is basically the opening bout of a game, designed to teach players about the combat mechanics and fighting systems. Cecilia always found these tedious and skipped right over the prologue.

I'm in trouble...

Her blood ran cold. A closer look revealed a gaggle of love interests, presumably selected as knights, standing behind Lean. In other words, it now looked like Cecilia had interrupted their very first group project (ha). Furthermore, ordinary people were incapable of subduing Obstructions, making Cecilia's identity all the more suspicious.

"Who are you?" asked Lean, her eyes widened in astonishment, as she stepped closer.

Cecilia's expression froze on her face.

"Here, Sister," whispered Gilbert.

"Huh?"

Cecilia felt something touch her left wrist and shivered at the cold metal sensation.

"Just act confident. That should work," her brother said.

Cecilia looked down at her wrist, where she saw the bracelet that was the sign of a knight—which must have originally been Gilbert's.

"But this is—"

"Oh? A knight has already performed his duty," came a voice from the stage.

"What?!" she yelped in a strained voice, watching as a man slowly descended from the platform and walked over.

"You performed a task fit for a knight and very admirably at that. It looked dicey there for a moment, but you did quite well. Keep using those skills of yours to protect the potential Holy Maidens."

"Hold on… What?"

He grabbed her hand and yanked her to her feet. The crowd broke into applause.

The most flushed and teary-eyed of all the onlookers were the members of the Prince Cecil Fan Club.

"You were wonderful, Prince Cecil!"

"Our prince is now a knight! He's gone even further out of our reach!"

"Your moves just now were simply amazing! Oh, I feel hot all over simply at the memory of it!"

Even the love interests, who had looked so suspicious moments ago, now nodded in understanding. Which made perfect sense. If Cecilia were a knight instead of an ordinary student, subduing an Obstruction would be well within the realm of possibility. Now that they could see the Sacred Artifact on Cecil's wrist, there was no need to suspect a thing.

Thanks to Gilbert's quick wits, Cecilia had evaded danger for the moment. But…

Doesn't this mean Gilbert bequeathed me his Sacred Artifact?!

The instant she realized that, all the blood drained from her face.

Her trials were only beginning.

✦ CHAPTER 2 ✦ First Romantic Event

"Someone, help! She's losing consciousness!"

Lean paled as she watched a student go berserk and attack a girl out of nowhere in the auditorium.

Next to her stood the school doctor, Mordred, ready to defend. On his wrist glinted a Sacred Artifact, one of the bands the envoy from the king had just brought in. He was a chosen knight.

"That's called an Obstruction. It's my first time seeing one, too, but I've heard they're demons who can possess people."

Another man stood at her side—Oscar, the crown prince of the nation. A Sacred Artifact was wrapped around his wrist as well. "I've also only read about them, but it seems they appear when the Holy Maiden's power is weakened. According to my reading, one appeared at the last Selection Ceremony, too, and the potential Holy Maidens and the knights subdued it."

"But who could the potential Holy Maidens be...?" she wondered, glancing around her. Even Lean, who'd been a mere commoner until recently, knew about them. She'd read picture books about the saints who defended the country from the shadows.

And candidates for Holy Maiden were here among the students. But the attack had broken out while the envoy was still in the middle of his explanation. No one knew who the prospective Maidens were yet.

"You're one of them," came a bright voice from behind her.

"I'm what?" she cried before they suddenly grasped her hand. An unnatural mark had formed there several days ago, shaped exactly like an oblong snowflake.

The person who'd taken her hand was a boy standing diagonally behind her. Along with his soft, short brown hair, he seemed just like a dog. Judging by where he was standing, he must have been in the same class as her.

"I'm Jade. I'm not sure why, but I think I've been chosen as a knight to protect you," he informed her, holding up his wrist to reveal the glittering silver bracelet on it.

"Um, so, Jade, why do you think I'm a Holy Maiden?" she asked hesitantly.

"You mean you didn't know? Before the Selection Ceremony for potential Holy Maidens, this floral mark appears on the candidates. And that means I am duty bound to protect you."

"Holy Maiden...," Lean repeated, utterly flustered.

Until recently, she'd been an orphan living in an almshouse; then she'd suddenly learned that she was a baron's illegitimate daughter and so had become nobility. And now she was a candidate for Holy Maiden on top of everything. Flustered was underselling it.

"In that case, we can get right to it. Let's take down that Obstruction together! Will you lend us your aid?"

"We need you to."

Mordred and Oscar gazed at her expectantly. In the face of their powerful stares, a sense of duty welled up from deep within Lean's heart.

"If you're sure I can help, then...," she answered, taking a step forward.

And then, miraculously, they completed their very first task.

That's the prologue to the original game, anyway.

"AAAAHHHHH! Why did my past self not take the prologue more seriously?! I should have memorized it! If I had, then this wouldn't have..." Cecilia moaned, head in her hands, lamenting how she'd stolen the great Lean's introductory spotlight and even acquired Gilbert's Sacred Artifact.

Next to her was, of course, Gilbert, an exasperated look on his face. It was lunchtime, and they'd brought sandwiches into their usual greenhouse and were now in the midst of a strategy meeting that was devolving into a pity party.

"It's in the past now, so there's no point beating yourself up over it. Also, if you don't eat fast, you'll be late for your next class," Gilbert insisted in an even more measured tone of voice than usual.

Cecilia glared at him through tears. "You don't understand the gravity of the situation, Gil!"

"And what would that be?"

"I told you, the Selection Ceremony is basically an election for the Holy Maiden candidates. I've now gotten one vote from you, which means I'm one step ahead of Lean! If she doesn't end up getting close to anyone else, I'm going to get picked to be Holy Maiden!"

And if that happened, bandits would attack Cecilia on her way to the church to receive her Holy Maiden baptism—and kill her. Then, bereft of their spiritual leader, Obstructions would overrun the country until it was destroyed.

That very unexpected ending made even Gilbert pull a face. "You'd die and the nation would go under..."

"Why do you look like that?"

"I'm just put off by the idea. You don't really think something so drastic would happen, do you?"

Up until now, Cecilia had only used vague words like *bleak outlook*, *total destruction*, and *tragedy* to describe her future to Gilbert. She'd never gone into specifics before, which was why he was so alarmed now.

The real mystery was actually why he'd helped her without knowing any of the details.

"So should I not have given it to you?" he ventured.

"No! I'm really grateful you made that snap judgment! If you hadn't, I might've been done for right then and there, to be honest!"

If Gilbert hadn't given her his Sacred Artifact, Cecil would have developed a reputation for being able to inexplicably exorcise Obstructions. Not only that, but there probably would have been a physical examination, which would have revealed Cecil as Cecilia. Then she would have had no choice but to become a candidate for Holy Maiden, putting her right on track for a route that would result in her inevitable ruin, no matter how hard she tried to reverse it.

So Gilbert's decision had absolutely been the correct one, and she was endlessly grateful to him for it.

She'd landed in this mess *entirely* because Hiyono Kanzaki, her past self, had skipped right over the prologue.

"I actually want to ask you, Gil, if you're sure about giving me your Sacred Artifact. I mean, that was your once-in-a-lifetime opportunity...," Cecilia mentioned, bemused, as she tilted her head to one side.

Being selected as one of the Holy Maiden's personal knights was the highest honor in the nation. They ranked higher than other members of nobility, only just below the king himself.

But Gilbert had handed his Artifact over to Cecilia, who had no intention of becoming Holy Maiden, which was tantamount to entirely throwing away those privileges.

"It's fine. I'm not really interested in power like that anyway... Besides, I wouldn't have felt like giving it to anyone but you in the first place," answered Gilbert, his cheeks full of sandwich. For some reason, that shook her a little. From the look on his face, he was clearly trying to hide his embarrassment.

Oh, right—Gil is a little shy around strangers. He only just met Lean, so he might not know how to approach her...

He'd been like this when they'd lived together in the Sylvie manor, too. El, the gardener who'd always brought Cecilia flowers; Hans, the soldier who'd taught them swordsmanship and martial arts; Donny, the butler's son who'd carefully looked after her—Gilbert had treated them all coldly. He made no attempt to get to know them and rarely looked at them even when he was conversing with them. Furthermore, he very much disliked Cecilia getting close to them, too.

The original game contains similar scenes. At first, this depressed shut-in categorically refuses to open up to Lean. When she takes it upon herself to help him with his studies, since he rarely attends class, she tries out all kinds of methods to get him to soften his heart around her. No matter how many times he rebuffs her, she never gives in, so ultimately, Gilbert relents and allows her kindness to slowly melt the walls around his heart.

"I must have loved you from the moment of our very first encounter. I think it was love at first sight. Thank you for pulling me out of that dark room. Thank you for opening up my world."

It was impossible to watch the scene where he reveals that he's fallen in love with her without crying.

Incidentally, choosing another love interest's route results in Gilbert's removal from the entirety of the narrative, probably due to his personality. He disappears as if he never existed to begin with, which his fans bemoaned across social media.

Cecilia gave her brother an encouraging pat on the shoulder. "You should be a little less shy while you're here at school!"

"Shy? What are you talking about?"

"I mean, you actually want to get to know Lean, don't you? Love at first sight! I know exactly how it feels to get tongue-tied around the person you like!"

"I don't understand what you're saying...," he replied, confused.

Cecilia beamed at him. "It's all right—just let your big sister handle this! Although, I don't want to have anything to do with Lean, so all I can really do is provide backup support. But anytime you need to talk, I'll give you advice! You can count on me!"

Gilbert said nothing in response. He just closed his eyes and shook his head wearily, the look on his face clearly betraying that Cecilia was a lost cause already.

They finished their sandwiches while idly chatting, then left the greenhouse. The area around it really was entirely deserted.

"Hang on—you said there were three candidates for Holy Maiden, including you. Who's the one besides Lean? You haven't mentioned her at all, so I'm a little curious," Gilbert said in a whisper, conscious of their surroundings.

After the tutorial battle, the royal envoy in the auditorium had once again asked all the students about the identities of the potential Holy Maidens.

Prodded by her suitors, Lean had hesitantly raised her hand. But no one else had named themselves.

Ordinarily, that would have been when Cecilia shoots her hand up, but since she certainly wasn't going to, the female students were sent to undergo physical examinations to check for the presence of a floral mark.

However, none of them possessed the mark, making Lean the Selection Ceremony's sole candidate.

Some students had been absent that day, and if a girl's mark had been in a feminine private place, then it would have been as good as invisible. The envoys had convinced themselves that the other candidates had refused to come forward, unwilling to handle the great responsibility of a potential Holy Maiden.

Cecilia frowned, tilting her head to one side in befuddlement. "Hmm. I don't actually know."

"What do you mean?"

"By this point in time, the other candidate for Holy Maiden should be dead."

"*Dead?*" Gilbert replied, his voice going hysterical.

In the game, there is indeed a potential Holy Maiden with an azalea mark on her skin. But she dies early on in the prologue.

A week before transferring into Vleugel Academy, Lean reads a news article about a murder case. The report says that the murder victim has an azalea mark on her shoulder. At first, Lean doesn't know how to make heads or tails of that detail, but once she arrives at school and finds out she is a candidate for Holy Maiden, the mark's significance becomes clear to her. When this fact dawns on the rest of the country, the authorities summon Lean and Cecilia and warn them to be on the lookout for someone targeting potential Holy Maidens.

Later in the game, some crimes occur that seem like the work of the Azalea Holy Maiden's murderer. They come to be known as the Killer.

"But I haven't heard anything about that, and I've been checking the newspapers. Not a single article on the murder has come out…," noted Cecilia.

"H-hold on a minute. This feels too much like someone is just waiting for our next move…," Gilbert stammered, clearly flustered, which puzzled her. "I only just heard that you could die if we keep going with this."

"Yeah, I did only just tell you," she admitted.

"And yet, now you're telling me that someone might be trying to murder you?!"

"What? Should I not have said anything?"

"I'm saying that you're informing me about this way too late!" Gilbert shouted, angrier than she'd ever seen him before. She blinked at him in shock.

In the game, Cecilia dies in two main ways. The first is via death penalty: She is punished for bullying Lean and/or harming someone.

The second is murder: Someone, possibly the Killer, does her in.

Unlike the death penalty ending, the details of her murder remain unclear, and the case goes unsolved.

The day after an attack on Lean, Cecilia is found stabbed in the chest with a knife, floating dead in a river, or hanged from a tree in a forest. The Killer is the suspect every time, and their motive is presumed to be Cecilia's candidacy for Holy Maiden.

Lending credence to this theory, an unidentified person who appears to be the Killer nearly assassinates Lean several times. But the main difference between her and Cecilia is that Lean survives the majority of these encounters.

Lean gets killed in a few bad endings, too, but in those instances, it is not the Killer but Cecilia who does the deed. Then she's decapitated in turn. Basically, if Lean gets murdered, then so does Cecilia.

"Why didn't you say anything until now?" Gilbert asked.

"I mean, you didn't ask…"

"This is something you should have brought up regardless! Why do you think I'm helping you?!" he roared in an earsplitting voice, causing Cecilia to cover her ears.

She really hadn't been trying to hide it. She'd just never had a chance to mention it.

"Well, forget it. It's not like you hid it on purpose… But in the game or whatever, do you ever find out the Killer's identity?"

"You do in the true love route, apparently…"

"But?"

"But I actually never got that far...," she admitted.

Gilbert heaved a sigh of obvious disappointment.

"I—I can't help it! I think I died before I could get to it!" she cried.

"But we can't come up with a strategy if we don't know who they are. What if they're targeting you?"

"I get that, but I'm not a candidate for Holy Maiden this time, so I don't think I..."

"You don't think you need to be all that careful? You're acting way too naive. Do you know the name of the candidate who gets murdered?"

"That never comes up once in the game..."

Gilbert let out another long sigh.

"That's something I really, really can't help!" she protested.

"I know. But does she have any defining characteristics besides her mark?" he asked.

"Uh...," she answered, sifting through her memories. In the game, the royal envoy displays a photo of the slain girl, but there's a mosaic overlay like frosted glass over it that makes it difficult to see.

But as she desperately combed through anything she could remember, they exited onto a path filled with students.

Right away, a thrilled voice shrieked loud enough for all to hear. "PRINCE CECIL!"

"Uh-oh...," she said under her breath, startled by the sudden cry and stumbling over her next step. A wall of female students instantly surrounded her.

The prince of the school now bore the title of renowned knight, which had driven them into a frenzy over their beloved idol. There was no way they were letting him go.

"Where were you? I wanted to have lunch with you..."

"I made you a lunch, Prince Cecil! I couldn't feed it to you today, but some other time is all right, too!"

"Ladies! You promised you wouldn't try to get ahead of one another, didn't you?! If Prince Cecil is going to eat with anyone, it's going to be with all of us!"

"Um, would you like to have some post-lunch coffee?"

"Not you, too!"

They just kept babbling, leaving Cecilia with a somewhat pained grin on her face. The girls were just like baby chicks whose parents had abruptly appeared bearing food. It was honestly always a pain that they crowded all together every time, but that didn't mean Cecil could treat them rudely. Cecil had to be the manliest and most gentlemanly of all…

From the topic of lunch, the conversation turned to singing the praises of how dashing Cecil had been in the auditorium earlier, which then sparked discussion on all kinds of other things.

Using a hand to stave off the crowd of girls excitedly attempting conversation, Cecilia pasted a charming, princely smile on her face. Then she reached out and traced a line down the jaw of the girl in front of her. "Don't twitter so much, little birds. I'd much rather listen to your sweet songs in turn."

(Translation: Speak one by one; I can't hear everything.)

At Cecilia's low-pitched voice, the crowd let out another round of squeals and screams.

From the edge of the throng, Gilbert was eyeing her coldly, predictably enough. "It's because you act like this that things escalate and get even more annoying to handle."

"Huh? What was that? Sorry, Gil—I didn't catch that."

"Nothing," muttered Gilbert after a pause, leaving Cecil to his crowd of adoring fans and heading to the classroom alone.

Cecilia was on the run.

From a younger student offering up some snacks.

From a classmate getting stubbornly handsy.

From an older student taking any opportunity to invite Cecil to spend the night with her.

"Ugh, this sucks! I seriously hate this!"

She was always on the run.

Two weeks after Cecilia screwed up in the auditorium, her fans' passion for the prince (?) who'd been selected as a knight had reached a fever pitch. Constantly chased around here and there, she had no time for herself at all. Someone would inevitably pop up next to her wherever she went and whatever she did.

It all came on so suddenly that she hadn't held another strategy meeting with Gilbert since their earlier one.

At first, Cecilia toughed out her lack of privacy and the need to constantly wear her princely smile. She knew that her fans' mania was fleeting, so she believed things would go back to how they'd been with the passage of time. But as the days wore on, Cecilia's tolerance for toughing it out hit its limit, leading to her current predicament of attempting escape.

"Prince Cecil, please wait!"

"I'm in a bit of a hurry now, sorry!" she said, shaking off the female students in hot pursuit and slipping into the courtyard. Worried cries of "Where did he go?" rang out as her pursuers passed right by but were unable to find her as she was camouflaged by the shadows of the thick hedges.

"Alone at last…" She sighed, leaning against a tree trunk. "I need to hook Lean up with someone, but I can never go anywhere in peace."

Since Cecilia had received a vote from Gilbert, she had to do whatever it took to get Lean and someone else to fall for each other so Lean could collect their Sacred Artifact. Lean and Cecilia were fortunately in the same class, so she'd thought it would be easy to instigate meet-cutes, but no matter how much she wanted to, she couldn't do a thing for the time being. It would be best to just let nature take its course with Lean's love life, but at the moment, there were no signs of developments. In fact…

"We need to change classrooms for our next lesson. Do you want to go together, Lord Cecil?"

"Lord Cecil, may I sit next to you?"

"Could you help me figure out this problem, Lord Cecil?"

Lord Cecil, Lord Cecil, Lord Cecil, Lord Cecil…

Why was Lean paying more attention to Cecil instead of her actual suitors? Yes, from her point of view, Cecil was a knight and therefore possibly a suitor, but there wasn't actually a Cecil route. The man himself didn't even exist!

I don't want to be cold to Lean, but I feel like if I don't, then Cecilia's life is going to wind up as Cecil's life…

Which would negate the entire reason she was dressing as a boy.

Well, the first three romantic events happen even if you don't manage to raise the suitors' affection points for you, so I guess I can think about it after that…

"Meow!"

"Meow?" she repeated, as a cry from behind interrupted her thoughts. She turned around to find a small cat. It had short legs and a coat that was a mixture of black and tawny brown. With its tottering, still-unsteady steps, the kitten was utterly adorable.

"Oh! You're so cute! Munchkin breed, maybe? So soft and fluffy!"

"Mrow," responded the kitten, who was evidently very used to humans, not resisting at all when Cecilia picked it up. She buried her face in its white belly. It smelled like sunlight.

"Oh my, looks like you have a little injury on your foot. Did you cut yourself somewhere? Wait just a second," Cecilia said, digging through her pocket and pulling out a light pink handkerchief, which she wrapped around the kitten's bleeding foot. "There we go! I'll take you by the nurse's office later. They might have some disinfectant. Oh, but can I put disinfectant for humans on you?"

"Meooow?"

"I'll ask Dr. Mordred. He's an intellectual-type character, so he should be able to answer just about any question!"

"Mrow!"

When she nuzzled the kitten's nose, it rubbed its head against her affectionately. Precious.

Just then, she heard talking from the other side of the hedge she was hiding in. One had a lovely, clear, and beautiful voice, while the other spoke in a deep, intimidating baritone. She recognized both.

Peeking through a gap in the hedges, she observed the speakers.

It was Oscar and Lean, gazing at the rosebushes.

Oscar Abel Prosper.

The nation's crown prince and fiancé to the duke's daughter, Cecilia Sylvie.

Eyes as sharp as knives flashed from beneath his deep scarlet hair. Despite his handsomeness, his expression gave off a cold impression. Tall and lanky, he exuded a characteristically royal aura.

Oh, yikes. We've gotten to this *part...*

She scrunched herself down so that they wouldn't find her. This was Lean and Oscar's very first romantic event.

In this scene, Lean—saddled with the heavy fate of being a potential Holy Maiden and all mixed up over it—encounters the crown prince Oscar in the courtyard.

"I know you've been saddled with a difficult role, but let's both do our best. At the very least, I think you're much more suited for

Holy Maiden than Cecilia. I find it very touching how you struggle through hardships instead of avoiding and ignoring them."

That is what Oscar says to encourage Lean, who is feeling entirely out of her depth.

Right, Oscar loves Lean from the moment he sees her. And he hates Cecilia more than anyone...

He views Cecilia as an incompatible fiancée, an archenemy who gets between him and Lean. Despite their engagement, he detests her more than anyone.

Cecilia, on the other hand, adores Oscar, and her jealousy leads her to hurt Lean. This incurs Oscar's wrath, which gets her imprisoned and then executed.

Actually, this "Cecilia hurts Lean, gets imprisoned, gets executed" plotline isn't exclusive to Oscar's route but appears rather often. In almost every route, it is Oscar who sends Cecilia to the gallows.

No matter who Lean ends up with, Oscar still holds feelings for her in his heart. What pure and unconditional love. But that love is also why Oscar abhors Cecilia in every single route.

Oscar is the one person I cannot interact with. Especially during this event...

In the next part of this romantic event, Cecilia butts in.

Things are just looking good between Oscar and Lean when Cecilia pops up from nowhere. Then she slaps Lean out of the blue and shouts at her.

"What do you think you're doing trying to seduce an engaged man, you shameless trollop?!"

Oscar admonishes Cecilia, saying, *"I could not be more disappointed in you,"* and leads Lean away with an arm around her shoulders. This incident spurs Cecilia to further hostility against Lean.

Because situations like that one keep cropping up, it leads

people to blame and suspect Cecilia of things she doesn't even do: *"It has to be her. That's the type of person she is."*

Okay! Time to make my escape! she thought. If she stayed here and interrupted this event by some chance, Cecil might end up with the same fate as Cecilia, ruining all her cross-dressing efforts.

From her crouch, she slowly rose to her feet.

But then the cat jumped from her arms.

"Aah!" she cried as the cat used her head as a springboard and leaped over to Lean and Oscar, of all people.

Meanwhile, the recoil from the cat's jump made Cecilia fall backward.

"Wha—?"

"Eek!"

Laid out flat with her back over the hedge, she tilted her head to sneak an upside-down glance at the couple.

N-now I've done it…

The cat burrowed itself in Lean's arms and let out a happy meow.

"Were you eavesdropping on us?" Oscar said, glaring down at Cecilia coldly. Her whole body was trembling. She'd definitely spoiled the mood as some random man intruding on his tryst with Lean.

Yes, about 80 percent of Oscar's affection points for Lean rest on this one scene.

If you like her so much, just give her your Sacred Artifact! she couldn't help thinking. But she had to play by the game's rules.

"Ah-ha-ha… It seems I've dozed off under this tree…," Cecilia-as-Cecil said, making up a desperate excuse.

"Oh…?" Oscar replied, narrowing his eyes. Naturally, he didn't believe it. *Crap.*

"Lord Cecil, are you all right?" asked Lean with an angelic smile as she helped Cecil up.

Ordinarily, Cecilia would be trying to avoid Lean at all costs,

but her smile was like the warm sun compared to the subzero frost Oscar exuded next to her.

"Thank you."

"I suppose even the gallant Lord Cecil has these moments. I feel like we might actually be quite similar," said Lean.

"O-oh really?"

"........."

So cold I think I'm going to get frostbite! Help!

Oscar stared at Cecil so hard he could bore a hole right through him.

Wh-what's his problem?! Is this like, "Don't get close to my Lean—who do you think you are?" *I'm not going to! I'm getting out of here!*

"Ah, I'll be heading back now. Very sorry for interr—"

"Would you like to join us for a chat? I'd actually love to get to know you better. Wouldn't you, Prince Oscar?"

"...I suppose."

Listen to that! Like hell he wants to!

"I-I'll have to take you up on that another time. Good-bye!" Cecilia blabbed, fleeing the scene and the cold gaze of the frosty tundra.

After Cecil left, the pair exchanged glances.

"He's gone. I wanted to talk to him more, though...," said Lean.

"Mmm. Besides that, he looks kind of familiar...," Oscar mused, falling into thought as he stroked his chin.

Then the kitten in Lean's arms gave a cute meow. It jumped down, which sent the handkerchief that was wrapped around its foot fluttering into the air.

"I think Lord Cecil brought this cat over. Hmm? It looks like it's hurt...," noted Lean.

"Guess he used a handkerchief to give it some first aid. It'll come right off if we leave it, so we should put a proper bandage on and disinfect the wound… Hang on. I've seen this handkerchief…," Oscar said, picking it up and furrowing his brow. He recognized it from somewhere.

"Who the hell is that guy…?"

A look of loathing on his face, Oscar glowered in the direction Cecil had fled.

When he'd been young, Oscar had not acted like a regular child at all.

It was drilled into him from the moment he was born that someday, he would bear the weight of the nation, so he thought of the people in his life as tools to help run the country. With such unthinkable pressure on his tiny shoulders, he grew up not relying on anyone for comfort and affection.

He never begged or asked the adults around him for anything—not his mother, the queen, nor the nanny who raised him. All he did was give orders.

Behaving like a little grown-up led the adults around him to decide he was steady and reliable, but they didn't hesitate to label him "impertinent" as well.

A high-handed, impertinent brat.

That described Oscar as a child.

And that was how he grew up in the royal palace, in persistent solitude.

After all, he was so put together in his attitude that his mother and nanny never interfered, nor did anyone try to get close to this authoritative, high-handed little boy. He also had no idea himself what he could be doing wrong, so year after year, he only grew lonelier.

Right around then, at the umpteenth society ball he'd gone to in his life, he met her. Cecilia Sylvie, the daughter of a duke. Oscar was six years old, and Cecilia was five.

She was the daughter of Duke Sylvie and very pretty, but rumor had it she was a selfish little girl whose parents spoiled her rotten. Oscar had only been born six months before her, so their ages were similar, and she was also of noble rank. On account of that, many people had good reason to whisper that she might become Oscar's fiancée.

While the adults were talking, she was focusing her undivided attention on her meal.

Freshwater fish à la poêle. Chicken confit. Minced pork. Colorful vegetable terrine. Braised beef. Grilled goat. Ratatouille, salad, soup…

Despite the fact that it was a stand-up meal served from a buffet, Cecilia paid that no mind, selecting one dish after another and ravenously devouring them at a table in the corner, as though she'd been starved for days.

True to her aristocratic upbringing, however, her table manners were impeccable and refined.

A society ball was no place to enjoy a meal; it was where nobles deepened friendships and exchanged information. So why, then, was she eschewing all conversation in favor of concentrating intensely on her food?

Since this intrigued him, he spoke to her. "Hey."

"Mmf?" she asked, fork in hand, as she turned around.

She looked so ridiculous that he felt his normally immovable facial muscles twitch.

Swallowing her mouthful of food, she cocked her head at him. "What is it?"

"What are you doing?"

"Eating, of course."

"I can tell that by looking at you. I'm asking you why you're doing it so greedily," he added, finally asking the question on his mind.

A shadow passed over her face as she looked down at her plate. "I'm stress eating."

"Stress eating?"

"I've been having a lot of dreams where I die lately. I know they're just dreams, and that's what I want to believe they are, but they just feel so real..." She sighed, her face somewhat drained of color. Then she went on, as if talking to herself, "I mean, if they're true, then I guess my life is over, and I'm just barreling toward the end of it. I don't want to accept that, but there's so many clear signs pointing to it being the truth, so sooner or later I need to steel myself for the worst. But I can't help raging inside my head against this fate..."

"I have no idea what you're saying."

"To put it simply, I might have a very bleak future, so I'm stress eating."

"Hey. I thought you were talking about bad dreams."

"I *wish* it was just bad dreams."

As they talked, he found he was totally losing track of the conversation. Paying him no heed, Cecilia gave him a bright smile. "But 'cause I get to eat all this yummy food, I've managed to distract myself quite a bit! This terrine was fantastic!"

"It was that good?"

"Yes! Oh, have you not tried it yet?"

"No, but..."

"That's a huge waste! The royal family is putting on this party, so we can take this chance to drink and eat to our heart's content! It's all free! All this delicious food for free!"

"...Do they not feed you at the duke's estate?"

A duke's daughter talking like money was any sort of concern made him worry that she was getting mistreated or something. But she shook her head with a smile. "Oh, of course they do. But since

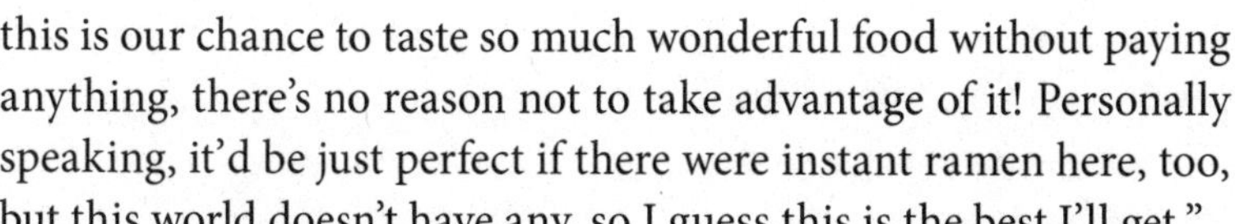

this is our chance to taste so much wonderful food without paying anything, there's no reason not to take advantage of it! Personally speaking, it'd be just perfect if there were instant ramen here, too, but this world doesn't have any, so I guess this is the best I'll get."

"Instant...ramen?" he repeated.

Cecilia gasped after a beat, the blood suddenly draining from her face. "Forget what I just said."

While he didn't really understand the "instant ramen" and the "this world doesn't have any" parts, neither did he get the impression she was a spoiled little girl from speaking to her. Instead, she seemed cheerful and innocent.

"Anyway, you'd be missing out not munching on any of this, so... Here. Try this," she encouraged, bringing a fork to his mouth out of nowhere.

"What?" He gasped, flummoxed. On the fork was a bite of the terrine she had just been raving about. Did she want him to eat off it?

Even his nanny had never babied Oscar like that. He turned red and took a step back. "Y-you're being very rude! I'm—"

"But it's good! Here."

"Mmmf..."

She stuck it in his mouth anyway. Feeling it would be improper to spit it out, he chewed and swallowed. Though it wasn't any different from the food he ate normally, the terrine was indeed delicious. But...

"It's really good, right?" she implored, smiling at him, and he felt his face soften.

Cecilia wasn't aware that Oscar was the crown prince. She probably thought he was some nobleman's young son, hence why she was taking such liberties with him. But getting treated with such affection made warmth bubble up in his chest.

"I guess," he admitted, his face flushing at her carefree smile. For someone who'd never had anyone he could call a friend, interacting with Cecilia was tantamount to his first experience playing with another child.

"Hee-hee," she giggled.

"What is it?"

"You got some sauce on you," she noted, using a handkerchief to wipe away the sauce on his cheek. "So careless. Kind of reminds me of Gil."

"You're the one who put it there." He balked, snatching the handkerchief from her and wiping it away himself.

She was still grinning at him. He asked, "What? Do I still have something on my face?"

"No. I was just a little worried about you because you seemed sort of sick, but I'm glad to see that your spirits have recovered. I knew yummy things could make us feel better!"

"...You thought I looked sick this whole time?"

"Yes. You were making this face like you were trying to pretend you didn't have a stomachache. At first, it was a bit scary."

"Trying to pretend I didn't have a stomachache...," he repeated. He hadn't really been frowning, just interacting normally with her. Now that she'd told him that he'd seemed as though he'd been bearing through a stomachache, he felt that he'd somehow lost some face.

"The face you're making now isn't scary at all. I quite like it," she added.

As he turned the word *like* around in his mind, he felt himself suddenly grow hot all over. Finding himself unable to look at her face, he dropped his gaze to the handkerchief she'd lent him. A clumsy-looking clover was stitched onto it.

"What is this?" he asked.

"Ah-ha-ha." She giggled. "I embroidered that. It was my first time, so I messed it up."

"...You're not very good."

"Guh…"

"But if you consider that there's room for growth, it's not that bad," Oscar encouraged, the gentle tone of his voice surprising even himself.

Cecilia's eyes rounded in shock. "Umm, about earlier—"

"Prince Oscar! There you are!"

Just as he was about to make an excuse, the cabinet minister came looking for him. He jogged over, his round body bouncing like a ball.

"What is it?" asked Oscar.

"His Majesty is calling for you."

"All right."

"O-Oscar…?" asked Cecilia in a trembling voice. He turned to see that she had gone completely pale. Her lips were quivering, and her big round eyes were opened even wider. "You're Oscar Abel Prosper?"

"Yes, and what of it?" he replied, nodding in assent as if to say, *You finally figured it out.*

Cecilia's eyes rolled back in her head, and she collapsed on the spot, frothing at the mouth.

That had been the last time Oscar had ever seen her.

He'd gone to the Sylvie manor to return the handkerchief he'd ended up borrowing, but he was told she was too ill for company. He came back to the manor on pretense after pretense after that, but the reception was the same. After that, rumors spread that she was in poor health, and she stopped appearing at society events altogether.

Now, twelve years later…

His grasp tightened around the handkerchief that did not differ much at all from the one Cecilia had offered him back then.

The inexpertly stitched clover was proof enough.

"Why does he have this handkerchief...?" he growled, hatefully recalling the boy everyone called the prince of the school.

"Cecil Admina, I need to talk to you," Oscar demanded, marching into the classroom first thing in the morning the day after his romantic event with Lean. Cecilia froze. Her classmates buzzed at the picture they made, the prince of the school juxtaposed against the actual heir to the nation.

"Wh-what is it?"

"It's hard to discuss in the classroom. Come here at lunchtime," he barked, slapping a note onto her desk. It jiggled with the impact. "I insist that you come. If you run away, I won't be responsible for what happens."

His eyes were as cold as ice as he glared down at her. In the face of that, all she could do was nod.

That lunchtime—

The meeting place written on the note was a reception room in the school, though it was not one that just anyone could use. It was a special one exclusively available to high-ranked members of nobility and their guests.

Since it was intended for socializing between nobles of high status, the room was quite spacious, with few partitions.

Seated on a sofa in the corner, Oscar showed Cecilia something. "Why do you have this handkerchief?"

"Handkerchief?" she repeated, looking down at what she'd tied around the cat's leg the day before.

Pointing to the edge of it, Oscar's voice took on a dangerous lilt as he asserted, "This is something I once borrowed from Cecilia."

"What?"

"I'll ask you one more time. Why do you have this?"

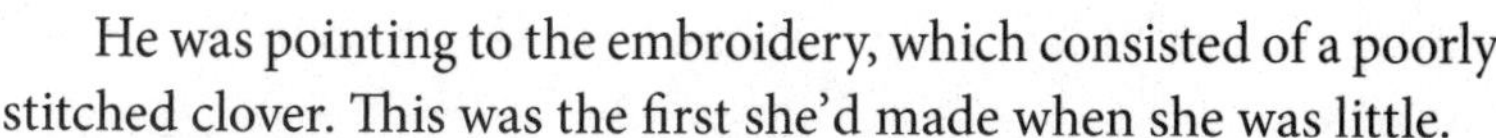

He was pointing to the embroidery, which consisted of a poorly stitched clover. This was the first she'd made when she was little.

I loaned this to Oscar...?

She desperately cast through her mind and managed to recall a memory from her childhood of a boy speaking to her.

"But if you consider that there's room for growth, it's not that bad."

A red-haired, sassy little boy breaking into a sweet smile that finally made him look his age, dispelling the pained look on his face. In his hand, he clutched a handkerchief meant to wipe his face. Along the edge was a misshapen four-leaf clover.

I seriously messed up!

Inside, Cecilia was freaking out. It was all coming back—how she'd once met Oscar at a high society party, and how afterward, she'd collapsed while foaming at the mouth. Then all the memories of her past life had returned to her with perfect clarity. But what she hadn't remembered was what had happened to the handkerchief she'd given him.

Which made sense because it happened twelve years ago.

I—I can't believe I'm going to get busted over this...

A chill ran down her spine. Oscar glared at Cecil silently.

Does he know?! Does he know Cecil and Cecilia are the same person?

"Um..."

"What is your relationship with Cecilia?"

"R-relationship?" she stammered, inwardly a little bit relieved to hear him say that. It didn't seem like he'd realized yet that Cecil equaled Cecilia. But it was obvious that depending on how she answered, he might very well start to suspect that possibility.

She chose her words very carefully. "Cecilia and I are friends..."

"A duke's daughter and a baron's son are *friends*?"

With that direct hit, she found herself completely stymied. Dukes and barons were just too far apart in prestige. Friendships among aristocrats generally only blossomed between those of similar rank.

And though it was conceivable that daughters of nobility could meet one another at a tea party, Cecil and Cecilia were a boy and a girl. Rationally speaking, it was impossible for them to be friends. In fact, it would have been more believable had she used the excuse that they were secretly together owing to their differences in social standing.

Needless to say, however, it would have been very alarming if the future queen of the country had a lover outside of the crown prince, so there was no way she could have gone with that…

Why are Oscar and I still engaged in the first place anyway?! You don't need a queen with weak health!

Naturally, queens who would give birth to the next generation of royalty needed to have strong, healthy bodies. That was why she'd continued to feign illness in front of her doting parents and why she'd done everything possible to establish herself as someone with a poor constitution. But her efforts still hadn't paid off.

Well, thanks to my frail and sickly reputation, I don't have to go to any more high-society parties, and none of the other nobles suspect a thing despite the fact that I still don't go to school…

"Are you *really* her friend?" Oscar asked, his suspicious tone drawing her out of her sea of thoughts and back into reality.

She fought to keep her face neutral. "Umm…"

"Your Highness, it would be more accurate to say that Cecil is *my* friend," cut in a very familiar voice from behind.

Cecilia whirled around to see someone she knew well. "Gil!"

"Isn't that right, Cecil?" Gilbert prompted.

"Oh! Yes!" she confirmed. Gilbert put an arm around Cecil, pulling him in toward him.

"Gilbert?" said Oscar.

"It's been a while, Your Highness. He—Cecil—is an old friend of mine, and my sister knows him through me," explained Gilbert.

"Gil, what are you doing here?" asked Cecilia.

"I came to your classroom to see if you wanted to eat lunch together, since we haven't in a while. Then I heard that the prince invited you to the reception room..."

A classmate must have sneaked a look at the paper Cecil received.

As the son of a duke, Gilbert was obviously entitled to enter the reception room. Once he'd heard about the situation, he'd run over to back his sister up immediately.

Gil! Thank you so much!

Cecilia even felt tears in her eyes.

"I see. So that means Cecil does have a connection to House Sylvie. But then, why are you carrying Cecilia's handkerchief?" Oscar pressed. Thanks to Gilbert's acting skills, Oscar seemed to believe that Cecil and Cecilia were acquainted with each another, but he still insisted on answers.

"W-well...," Cecilia hedged.

"My sister lent it to him. She and Cecil get on well, so they've spent some time together," answered Gilbert.

"But she's always absent from society parties," Oscar pointed out.

"As you know, she is in weak health. Though she's technically enrolled in this academy, she's rarely well enough to attend. They mainly met up with each other at home," deflected Gilbert smoothly.

Cecilia's eyes bugged out as she listened to her brother spouting lies as naturally as he breathed. She could never have done that so deftly.

"I've asked to come over and see her many times myself but have never managed. So then why has *he* seen her?" demanded Oscar.

"Surely that's because Cecilia doesn't fully trust Your Highness. Perhaps she even dislikes you," suggested Gilbert.

Crck... There came the sound of fissures cracking open across stone. Suddenly, Cecilia realized the two men were glaring daggers at each other, completely ignoring her even though she was the topic of conversation.

"Oh? You think Cecilia doesn't like me?" Oscar hissed in a threatening tone.

"I couldn't say definitively, but that does seem like the only explanation," Gilbert said acidly. "And as I've insisted to you many times before, she isn't strong enough physically to be the queen. Won't you consider just breaking off the engagement already?"

"That's not something you have the right to object to, Gilbert. The qualities that determine aptitude for becoming queen include intelligence, grace, and breeding. I can't deem her unfit for the title simply because her body is a little on the weak side," Oscar shot back.

As invisible sparks crackled between the two of them, she felt her facial muscles twitch involuntarily.

Why are these two getting into a fight? And besides, it feels like they've fought about this a million times before...

Unlike Cecilia, who was purportedly too ill to attend them, Gilbert had made many appearances at society gatherings as the next head of House Sylvie. That must have been where they'd come across each other in the past.

While she ruminated on that, the two boys' verbal sparring match was kicking into high gear.

"Still, it seems to me that physical health is most important, considering the heavy burden of giving birth to and raising the next king," Gilbert insisted.

"The queen's role is more than simply bearing children, isn't it? I've thought this for a while, Gilbert, but aren't you a little overly dependent on her? I suspect you have a sister complex."

"Better that than someone clinging to a memory that's over ten years old now. And most importantly, my sister and I are family, while she and Your Highness are strangers. Isn't it the most ordinary thing in the world for a brother to worry about his sister?"

"Strangers? Cecilia and I are engaged."

"Don't you mean engaged *for now*?"

"Can you really claim you're family anyway? You're only adopted in!"

"I regret to inform you that I consider that to be the greatest thing about our relationship. I don't view my past as a negative in the slightest."

No longer able to keep pace with their conversation, Cecilia looked from one to the other with a look of dismayed concern on her face.

I guess I've learned that these two are unexpectedly close, at the very least.

This was the first time she'd ever seen Gilbert have so much to say, as well as the first time she'd seen Oscar get so emotional. She had no doubt that this was a habitual argument only they could understand that took place in their own little world.

This is a perfect example of friends who are always arguing! Cecilia concluded. She'd always tended not think too deeply about things she didn't immediately understand.

"I suppose you may be correct. We haven't seen each other in more than ten years, so of course she could be avoiding me," Oscar murmured hatefully, giving the handkerchief back to Cecilia.

But just as she reached to take it, Oscar grabbed her wrist and pulled her in close to him.

"Aah!"

"Your Highness!" Gilbert cried, immediately trying to stop him, but Oscar held him at bay.

In a low voice, he growled in Cecilia's ear. "Cecil."

"Y-yes?!"

"Have you seen Cecilia recently?"

"I—I guess…," she admitted, reasoning that she saw herself in the mirror every day. That had to count.

Oscar's lip curled at her vague affirmation. "I have a favor to ask."

"Yes?"

"Arrange for me to see her. Any way you can."

Anyone could recognize that as a clear and obvious order—with a threatening edge.

✦ CHAPTER 3 ✦ Outdoor Education

The grounds were awash with green, new leaves freshly adorning the trees. Gentle sunlight shone down on the students as they chatted and conversed in crystal clear air. A soft breeze caressed their cheeks, the floral scent it brought tickling their noses.

Today's weather was absolutely perfect for picnics—as clear and temperate as could be.

So then why have I ended up in this situation?

"Cecil, where are we with that thing I asked you to do?"

"……"

Caught between a firm, manly chest, and a wall as white as chalk, Cecilia broke out in a cold sweat.

Threatening her was Crown Prince Oscar, his handsome face screwed into a scowl. His right hand was planted firmly on the wall behind her, pinning her against it—a classic move from all her favorite dating sims.

"That thing I asked you to do" referred, of course, to Oscar's order—excuse me, *request*—that Cecil arrange for him to meet with Cecilia.

A forced smile on her face, Cecilia scratched at her cheek. "Ah, well…"

"Not yet?"

"I mean, you can't really say 'yet' since you only just asked me the day before yesterday...," she hedged.

This prince was too impatient. He'd also summoned Cecil yesterday and had given him the exact same treatment. At this point, it was all but certain he'd keep calling Cecil out and trapping him against a wall until he'd managed to set a date for Oscar's meeting with Cecilia.

C'mon, give me a break here... Cecilia sighed inwardly. While her original goal of having absolutely nothing to do with Oscar was already out the window, she still didn't want to get too close to him if at all possible.

"Also, I want to clarify this one more time... Are you *really* Cecilia's friend?" Oscar pressed.

"I told you before..."

"So let me get this straight: It's possible for you, a guy who only cares about being popular with the ladies and just thinks with his dick, to behold the purest of angels and *not* make a pass at her?"

Why's this dude romanticizing me like that? And wow, his opinion of Cecil is at rock bottom...

Her regard for Oscar was dropping fast. Well, not that it was ever that high to begin with...

"She's really just a friend, Your Highness," Cecilia insisted, arranging her features into a pleasant smile.

Oscar's eyebrows only knit even closer together. "Don't call me that. Just Oscar is fine. And don't be so polite with me."

"Uh..."

"When I meet with Cecilia, I don't want her to think of me as someone who makes his own friends call him 'Your Highness.'"

Picky, picky...

Her esteem of him had now dipped into the negatives.

Oscar, a head taller than Cecil, looked down on him imperiously. "Just hurry it up and set up a spot where we can m—"

All of a sudden, Oscar abruptly faltered, and Gilbert appeared behind him.

She realized that Oscar had fallen to his knees; apparently, Gilbert had struck the back of Oscar's knees with his own, forcing them to bend.

"What are you doing to Cecil, Your Highness?" he asked.

"Gilbert!" Cecilia cried.

"I told you that it's pointless to threaten Cecil, and I've also said many times that you should go through me if you want to see Cecilia..."

"If I did that, you'd never let me see her!" roared Oscar.

"Why are you talking about this like it's going to happen? Of course you're not going to get to see her."

"Listen here, you little—"

Oscar lunged at Gilbert, attempting to grab him by his lapels. Gilbert brushed him off as if he were a particularly annoying fly. He was clearly used to this.

This is pretty different from how they were in the game...

There, they don't interact much at all. Gilbert's reclusive nature aside, Oscar should have no reason to get involved with him. Personality-wise, the Oscar of the game is more the cool and collected type; he's much more mature than his age would suggest. And as a perfectly composed prince, he also takes an extraordinary amount of pride in his royal status. He doesn't act like a typical teenager at all. Or he doesn't in the game, at least...

What had changed him?

I guess this does make interacting with him easier, though.

Oscar and Gilbert were still staring daggers at each other.

"Do I need to remind you that you're going to be my subject once I'm king?"

"But we're still in school right now. Don't you think it's possible my sister is uninterested in seeing you because you're always saying petty things like that?"

"Guh..."

"Moreover, I believe it should be impossible for you to run the country without the support of the Sylvies. And yet, you regard me as a lowly subject?"

"I never said I see you as lowly!"

"I'll give you credit for that, Your Highness. That's one thing about you I don't hate."

"Then—"

"But that has nothing to do with whether or not I give you access to my sister," Gilbert asserted. He seemed to have gotten the upper hand.

Realizing that he couldn't win this war of words, Oscar ground his teeth in frustration. "That's why I didn't ask you! I asked Cecil!"

Oscar's gaze landed on Cecilia. "You'll do it, won't you?"

"I-I'm handling it—"

"Your Highness, that's a threat—"

"Shut up! Cecil said it's fine, so it has nothing to do with you!"

Gilbert let out a deep sigh. With all this childish bickering, you'd think Oscar was the younger one.

"Fine. But could you sort that out later? I came here because I have business with Cecil," Gilbert stated, pulling Cecil out of Oscar's grasp.

"What business? Lunch?" asked Cecilia.

He whispered, "That, too—but apparently, there's been a bit of a development with Lean, so I came to tell you about it."

She jolted at that news.

"I caught it by chance in the courtyard, so I wanted to tell you if you didn't know about it," he explained, his face softening into a little grin.

Gilbert led her to the courtyard, which Lean was indeed occupying. She was standing across from a boy.

Cecilia stared at them from the shadows. "Is that Jade?"

"Jade Benjamin. He was chosen as a knight, wasn't he?"

Unusually for a student at the elite Vleugel Academy, Jade Benjamin was a young entrepreneur born to a commoner family. Since the Benjamin family had their hands in an extensive range of industries throughout Prosper, it wouldn't be exaggerating to say that they controlled the country's economy. In honor of their accomplishments, the king had awarded them the title of baronet last year.

Belying his status as a young businessman, Jade had an easygoing nature and a cute, puppylike charm, which made him a fairly popular character.

"See? They look pretty cozy, don't they?" Gilbert whispered into her ear.

"They really do," she agreed, nodding.

Jade and Lean were talking to each other, matching blushes on their faces. It was even more touching that they'd chosen a place without many other people around.

"You've been run ragged by so many different things lately, so I thought you might perk up if I told you about this."

"Gil! Such a good boy, thinking of your sister!"

"Yeah, yeah."

What a blessing it was to have a little brother who was so conscientious of his sister.

So as not to waste her brother's good judgment, Cecilia focused all her attention on Lean and Jade.

Self-consciously, Lean drew out a notebook she'd hidden in her school uniform and handed it to Jade. Her shy, crimson complexion was the picture of a young girl in love.

"So is this one of those 'events'?" asked Gilbert.

"Yup. This is the fourth event, which only occurs if his affection points have reached a certain level! The Heart-Throbbing Secret Diary Exchange event!" Cecilia whispered back excitedly.

While a character's first three events happen regardless of affection points, it's a different story starting from the fourth event. From then on, they won't trigger unless there's a certain level of mutual trust and companionship between the characters.

"Since the Heart-Throbbing Secret Diary Exchange is happening so soon, that must mean Jade is Lean's favorite! That's good news!"

"Not that I care, but you thought up that event name, didn't you?"

"Oh, you can tell?"

"Because it's so lame," Gilbert teased, smirking as he fired off a sassy remark. What happened to the respectful tone he'd taken with Oscar?

"Okay, so what kind of event is this?" he asked, starting over. Cecilia scanned through her mental records of how Lean and Jade fall in love.

In the game, Lean and Jade have a pretty good relationship from the start. Not only were they classmates, but they had also both been commoners originally, so they shared many values and philosophies. It really was inevitable that they would grow closer.

But this very intimacy invites teasing from their classmates. Unable to handle the embarrassment, Lean distances herself from Jade. That's when he invites her to meet with him privately before giving her that notebook.

"Do you want to make a secret all our own?"

Jade whispers that to her, lips parted in a smile. For the first time, Lean sees him as more than a friend. After that, they start writing secret letters to each other in the notebook.

"Jade's route is heavy on mystery elements, so that notebook comes in handy there!"

"Hmm."

"Gil, you don't seem very interested."

"I mean, I don't care all that much about other people's love lives to begin with," he admitted.

Gilbert Sylvie was the enemy of all fans of the dating sim genre.

But despite that, he still cared enough to listen to her talk about it, meaning he was doing this entirely for her sake. She couldn't thank him enough.

After chatting happily for a little while longer, Lean and Jade went their separate ways.

Cecilia emerged from the shadows, a spellbound look on her flushed face. "Ah, I got to see something wonderful. Let's start by throwing everything into helping them get together!"

It didn't matter who gave Lean their Sacred Artifact as long as she had one, which would make Cecilia safe for the time being. That was her most pressing goal right now.

"We're about to go on the school camping trip! I've gotta do something to make sure that event succeeds!" she enthused, all worked up. Then she noticed a piece of paper where Lean and Jade had just been. She walked over and picked it up. It was a scrap that had been torn from their notebook.

"What's THIS?!" she cried, squeaking out the last word.

"What did you find?"

"Gil! Don't come over here!"

"What?"

"Just don't!"

Holding out a hand to stop him from walking over, Cecilia scanned the contents.

I wrap my arms around his back, savoring the feel of him.

His heart is beating so fast. That alone makes me so happy I could cry.

"Why are you crying?" he asks. Only then do I realize that I have started to weep.

He's so adorable, he makes me feel crazy—like my heart is filled with so many emotions it's about to burst open.

For the very first time, I recognize that this is love.

I'm in love with another boy.

An exquisite feeling of guilt surges up inside me. But I can no longer stop myself from feeling the way I do about him.

I press him down, tracing his jawline with my thumb.

Then his lips—

"Cecilia?"

"Waaaauuugghhhh! Don't come up behind me!"

She'd found a fanfic. Not only that but one that belonged to a certain genre starting with a *B* and ending with an *L*.

Not only *that*, but it was so dirty that it almost qualified as explicit content!

Shaking her head furiously, Cecilia hid the scrap of notebook paper behind her. "You're not ready for this!"

"I don't understand..."

"You don't need to! Don't enter this hell! Once you're in it, you're in it for life!"

If you asked Cecilia in her past life, as Hiyono, if she were a BL fangirl, her answer would be a resounding no. She simply enjoyed all romance stories, BL included. She had neither prejudice nor preference.

Although she'd just mentioned BL hell, that was just a term she'd picked up from a friend of hers who could find romance between men in any anime series, manga, or book she consumed. Her friend had been a BL fangirl through and through—so utterly corrupted that she had been able to concoct M/M pairings even in dating sims where the point was to play a girl dating men. She could even find gay pairings in inanimate objects.

Bright and full of energy, she'd been true to her own desires and a ton of fun to be around.

"But why would this be here…?"

The wind must have blown out a scrap from the notebook. How very negligent. This was a toxic substance that required careful handling.

So there are girls who like BL in this world, too…

What an unlucky girl to be born into the world of a girl's dating sim of all things.

As Cecilia ruminated on the girl's misfortune, she heard her friend's voice in her head:

"All the guys in dating sims for girls are beautiful, so it's easy to pair them off with one another. Oh! I want to get reborn into a dating sim world!! That way I can spend my entire life gazing at hotties!!"

"Perhaps she's not so unlucky after all." Cecilia snorted before she realized it, caught up in the memory of her friend's voice.

"Hiyono! Read my latest fic!"

She loved creating. On top of drawing and writing fan fiction, she even went so far as to make her own original games.

"Come on. Your fics are good, Ichika, but why do you make them all BL? At least write a guy-girl pairing for once if it's for a dating sim!"

She was cheerful and lived life to the fullest. I loved her.

I couldn't quite get on board with the full depth and breadth of her interests, but as a reader, I still enjoyed her creations.

"Don't be ridiculous. BL pairings shine even more brightly in the world of dating sims!"

"That's a little too advanced for me. I'm not sure I get it."

"Forbidden love scorned by the rest of the world! Your crush is head over heels for the heroine! But the heroine is head over heels for you! The jealousy that arises from that, and the obsession that follows! And then—love!"

"Why does it turn into love there?"

"If they hate each other, that's already love! Enemies to lovers means that once they're enemies, they're practically dating!"

"Uh—Wha...? Can you speak in a language normies can understand?"

While the way her mind worked sometimes overwhelmed me, we got along oddly well and were always hanging out together.

Even though we were headed for different colleges after graduation.

Even though she was going to move away.

Despite all that, we were inseparable. We promised each other that we would be friends forever, even after graduating high school and starting a new chapter of our lives.

Yes, we were together even then.

"Hiyono, you're going to see this movie, right?"

"Holy Maiden 3?"

"Yup! It's so exciting to see a dating sim for girls get a movie adaptation!" she shouted, jumping up and down.

"That doesn't happen all that often, huh? Even though a lot of them get made into anime series."

"Exactly! And I really love the director, so I have high hopes for this one!"

"You're really into them, right, Ichika?"

"Someday, I want us to work together!" she cried, eyes sparkling as she talked about her dreams for the future.

She was so bright it was blinding; I had to squint a little against the glare. "Wow. So you've already got your sights set on something."

"Hee-hee. Oh, so anyway, do you want to see it with me?"

"Sure. When?"

"After school today!"

And then the movie theater caught on fire.

Ichika was desperately trying to carry out the person next to her, who had fallen unconscious.

"Ichika! We can't stay here!"

"No! I can't just leave her here! You go out first, and I'll follow!"

"But—"

"If you don't hurry, you'll pass out, too!"

"I can't leave you, Ichika!"

I wasn't as nice as her. If I were to weigh my own life against a complete stranger's, I couldn't place them above myself.

But I couldn't leave Ichika. She and I had promised to be friends forever.

I grabbed hold of the unconscious woman's other side.

Petrifying heat swept my cheeks, and burning flames licked at us mercilessly.

"Hurry, we have to get out!"

But the exit she pointed to was already engulfed in a blaze.

My skirt caught fire, so I slapped at the flames desperately. Then the sleeve on that arm also caught fire.

"Ichika!" I cried beseechingly, but when I turned to look, she was lying unconscious on the floor.

"Ichika! Ichika! ICHIKA!"

I shouted her name frantically, but she wouldn't answer me.

Her lungs were full of smoke.

Finally, my consciousness went black, too, and I plunged into the abyss.

"AHHHHHH!"

Cecilia shot up in bed with a scream. Beads of sweat rolled from her forehead down her cheeks, landing on her hands.

She'd had a dream. A truly horrendous dream.

A burning, tragic, and heartrending nightmare.

"But what was I dreaming about...?"

Only the bitterness remained as the rest of the vision faded away. She'd forgotten it.

"It was probably the same thing as always..."

A recurring nightmare had plagued her ever since recovering memories of her past life. Though she could never quite remember its contents, it was easy to deduce it wasn't pleasant, because she always woke up from it drenched in sweat, pain lancing through her heart.

She theorized that this repeating nighttime vision must have been Hiyono's last moments.

That, in turn, meant that the pain in her heart had to be regret. In those dreams, perhaps she remembered Hiyono's frustration at being robbed of a full, long life.

"But I've gotten a second chance at life and everything. This time, I've gotta make it a happy one! Like hell am I gonna die in the middle of it like Cecilia does in the game!"

She pressed a fist to her breast with renewed determination.

Then her eyes landed on the clock. It was eight fifteen.

"Oh crap, I'm gonna be late! And for the trip orientation meeting!"

From the next day on, Cecilia and the other second-years at the academy would be heading into the woods for an extended outdoor education trip. Today was the orientation.

Quick as a flash, *she* transformed into *he*, grabbed her schoolbag, and flew out of the dorms.

The school field trip.

This was one of the academy's major events. During the trip, the students would stay at lodges in the mountains and highlands for a few days. There, they would learn the joys and struggles of communal living, developing outdoor skills like tent pitching, campfire starting, and orienteering.

Why...?

Amid the clean, fresh air and the verdant trees and nature, Cecilia was trembling with anxiety.

Why is this happening to me...?

In her right hand, she clutched a note that read "3," while her left hand was clenched in a fist. Most of the boys in front of her were whooping with joy. A few looked dejected as well, though Cecilia's predicament was on a whole different level compared to theirs.

And next to her…

"So you're my roommate, huh? Well, I suppose that's better than living with a complete stranger," remarked Oscar, who was also holding a paper marked "3."

Let's rewind to a few hours earlier.

Cecilia and the other Vleugel Academy second-years had ridden for three hours in horse-drawn carriages until they'd arrived at a high, open plain. Their destination, of course, was the academy's outdoor campus. They would be staying in one big lodge, just like in the dorms. But it came with a catch.

Normally, each student would receive a single room in the lodge, but there were a few more male students than there were rooms. This wasn't a mistake on the academy's part; it was deliberately designed so that some of the male students would end up rooming together.

As a girl dressed as a boy, Cecilia would obviously be exposing herself to certain dangers if she were to share a room with another person. But she'd underestimated the chance of that happening, reckoning that only a very small number of the boys would have to share. She wouldn't get picked.

But when they'd drawn lots to determine dorm assignments, she'd pulled none other than the exact same number as Oscar.

And why is it him, of all people?!

Face tight with tension, she unconsciously crushed the note in her fist.

Someone tapped on her shoulder, and she turned around to find her classmate Jade, looking on with concern. "Cecil, are you okay? You don't look so good…"

"Jade…"

"Are you nervous because you're going to room with the prince?"

"Uh, sure," she replied, nodding vaguely, her face pale.

Ever kind and considerate, Jade patted her back as he whispered, "Do you want to trade with me, then?"

"Really?!" she cried, her head popping up. Jade should have a single. It would be a lifesaver if he was willing to trade.

Jade smiled, his eyes crinkling up. "Yeah. I have some things I'd like to talk to him about anyway."

His angelic, puppy-dog smile was almost blinding. She thanked all the gods, including her newest one, Jade.

"Then pl— Oh, wait!"

She interrupted herself, realizing she couldn't trade at this stage.

Lean and Jade were going to have a romantic event here that absolutely could not be skipped. And for that to happen, it was vital that Jade have a single.

The boys draw lots to decide room assignments in the game, too, and Lean and Jade's trust points determine whether he draws a double or a single. Without enough affection points, Jade would get a double, eliminating any chances of a romantic event.

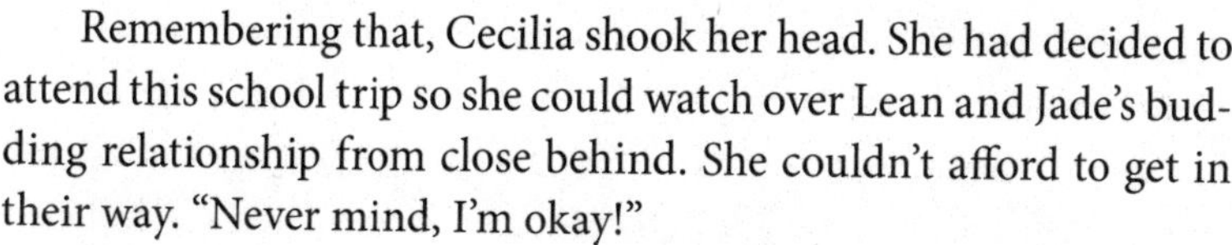

Remembering that, Cecilia shook her head. She had decided to attend this school trip so she could watch over Lean and Jade's budding relationship from close behind. She couldn't afford to get in their way. "Never mind, I'm okay!"

"But…"

"I like Oscar, so I'm really fine with it!"

After an awkward pause, Jade replied, "I see." Then he nodded. "Let me know if you change your mind."

She hadn't interacted much with this classmate of hers up until now, but true to the game, Jade was a really good guy. She couldn't help but pray with all her might that he and Lean would fall in love soon.

"Guess I can't worm my way out of this one. I'll just have to figure something out myself," she sighed, giving up on the idea. In life, where there's a will, there's a way.

While the lodge featured large public baths where most students would bathe, she'd also read that each room came equipped with its own shower. Plus, it wasn't like she and Oscar would be sleeping in the same bed. She should be able to keep His Obtuseness fooled for a night or two.

Heart full of optimism, she entered their shared dorm.

And found herself aghast.

Uh, this is a lot more cramped than I expected.

The lodgings back at the elite Vleugel Academy were fairly large. In addition to a bedroom, they came with two more rooms. One was a simple kitchen stocked with cookware, though most students wouldn't have any use for it. The other held a desk, a closet, and even a hand-crank telephone for emergencies.

But the dorms in this lodge looked more like the tiny Japanese hotel rooms from her past life. Save for a bunk bed replacing the standard hotel single bed, they were virtually identical.

Not only was it small, but it was also limited to a single living space, and the furniture consisted solely of a desk and two chairs. The closet they would presumably share was barely big enough to fit Cecilia herself. Incidentally, closets in the Vleugel Academy apartments were roomy enough for three or four bionic robot cats to inhabit.

"Y-yikes," she said.

Relaxing here would be even harder than she'd anticipated. They would be out of the room all day doing outdoor activities and would only come back to sleep, so it wasn't exactly *unreasonable*, but the diminutiveness of the space still concerned her.

Being trapped with him all the time in this shoebox meant she could never take off her wig. Or her binder. "And it gets so sweaty and tight…"

"Did you say something?" Oscar asked, turning back to her with the key in his hand.

"Nothing at all!" she chirped, shooting up with her spine ramrod straight.

Fortunately, each bunk had curtains along the perimeter that could be drawn for privacy once in bed. That at least meant she'd only be bothered by the wig until bedtime, which was one saving grace. Perhaps the only one.

Well, I'll figure out all the little details later. The more important thing is getting Jade and Lean together! she thought with determination, steeling her resolve.

Dearest sister,

How's camping? Are you having fun?
You're so wild and scatterbrained that I do find myself worried about the idea of you set free in nature.

You're not causing anyone any trouble, are you?
Or doing anything dumb?
If you end up roommates with anyone (worst-case scenario being the prince) and your cover is in danger of getting blown, contact me at once.
I won't let anyone stop me from coming to your aid.

Gilbert

"Is my little brother psychic?"

"Cecil, did you say something?" asked Oscar from behind her.

"N-nope, nothing!" she replied, hiding the letter. Cecilia had discovered it tucked away in her bag when she'd unpacked her things. She had no idea when he'd slipped it in there, and as she unfolded it, a little half smile came to her lips.

Gilbert had been vehemently opposed to Cecilia attending the school camping trip from the very beginning. Vleugel Academy's outdoor education program was entirely optional, so not every student attended. The communal living aspect made it especially dangerous for Cecilia, so she initially hadn't planned on going. But since Lean and Jade had gotten so close all of a sudden, she'd decided to tag along to observe their progress.

Gilbert tried to dissuade her up until the moment she boarded the carriage, reminding her that the potential pitfalls far outweighed any benefits. Slipping that letter into her bag was his final way of protesting her decision.

Gil really has such a soft spot for his big sister.

Although he'd voiced his objections loud and clear, and in a way that was not exactly endearing at that, his love and concern for her still showed through in his overall message. From a perverse angle, it was almost impressive that the Cecilia of the game could bring herself to mistreat such an adorable creature.

But if I write him now, he'll worry again. I have to make it through this fix I'm in on my own!

"Cecilia, you're amazing for managing to conceal your secret and not letting the prince suspect a thing. And all while sharing a room with him! My opinion of you has totally changed!"

Cecilia grinned to herself as she fantasized about how Gilbert would react once she returned triumphant from the trip after navigating this sticky situation.

That's because you only ever see me at my most helpless and unreliable! Now's my chance to restore my image!

Cecilia nodded, caught up in a train of thought that would have undoubtedly made Gilbert blow a gasket were he there in the flesh.

There was no longer anyone who could stop her.

"Hey. Are you done unpacking?" Oscar asked.

"Oh—yeah," Cecilia replied, pasting on a friendly smile. Oscar got angry if she spoke to him too politely, so she was trying to use more casual language like she would with a friend, but it still felt a little stiff.

Apparently, he'd also demanded that Gilbert—who spoke to him in unfailingly formal and polite tones—be more casual with him as well. But Gilbert had stubbornly refused: *"I certainly will not."*

"We have to go get lunch ready now. Let's go."

"Okay," Cecilia said, following Oscar out of the room.

Lean and Jade's event at the school camping trip hinges entirely on their exchange diary.

Though it has been a while since they'd started the diary, Lean still feels as much hesitation as ever about acting congenially with Jade face-to-face.

She longs to grow close to him. But the fear of incurring further bullying from her classmates, coupled with the fear that Jade would dislike her if he got to know her, keeps her at bay. All that is on her mind when Jade writes, *"Let's sneak out of the lodge tonight,"* in their exchange diary.

Together, they slip away and spend a romantic evening chatting and stargazing. Jade is unexpectedly informed about astronomy and entertains her with stories of other countries' myths about the constellations.

These two friends are close enough to be almost no different than lovers. As they while away the hours, occasionally one or both of them blushes.

That's when a scream erupts from the lodge, spoiling the intimate mood. They dash over to the lodge, only to find it under assault from Obstructions—a possessed classmate and aggressive feral dogs.

Hastily, they pitch in to help, but Jade gets injured in the fight while protecting Lean.

Incredibly anxious about him, Lean volunteers to nurse him back to health for the duration of their stay at the lodge. It's here where her true feelings for the boy begin to dawn on her, and vice versa.

In other words, this event has gotta happen!

Lost in memories from her past life, Cecilia brought down a cutting knife on a potato with vigor. The cutting board shook with a loud *bang*. But all she'd managed to cut off was a bit of the peel.

"Tch. Got away from me, huh?" she muttered ominously, lifting her knife up again. When she swung it down as hard as she could, it cracked the cutting board and sent pieces of potato flying. She promptly dodged the wayward vegetable chunks, but one slightly grazed her cheek, and she felt a stinging pain.

"Why, you little—"

She rubbed at her cheek with her sleeve, which left it with a red smudge. Blood.

"You've got some nerve cutting me, you lowly root vegetable..."

She was making curry.

"I'll make you rue the day you dared to wound me!"

Just making curry.

The next time she lifted the knife, someone grabbed her wrist, immobilizing it. She turned back to see Oscar, visibly disconcerted. "Sorry to break up your fun, but what do you think you're doing?"

"Chopping potatoes, obviously," she answered after a pause.

"So *not* playing around?"

"Yes, not playing around."

The next thing she knew, Oscar had confiscated her knife and cutting board.

"Hey, those are mine!" she protested.

"Maybe try looking around you!" he snapped. When she did, she saw the other students gawking at her in fear. Even the usual giggly, squealing bunch of girls were all pale-faced.

"Huh? But why?"

"*Why?* You were standing there with a truly terrifying scowl plastered across your face while muttering to a potato! That's enough to scare anyone!"

"I guess they heard me talking to myself..."

"You talk to yourself that way?" Oscar sighed. "You're bad at cooking, aren't you? Despite your reputation for good grades and athletic abilities."

"Ah-ha-ha... Yeah, cooking's the only thing I just can't manage...," she admitted.

Hiyono also hadn't been much of a chef. While she wasn't proud of it, she'd once tried to prepare a meal for her mother—and had gotten banned from the kitchen for the rest of her days. It wasn't that she didn't care about cooking or couldn't judge taste. She was simply uncoordinated—all thumbs, pretty much.

Even as Cecilia, she'd once asked the chef to let her make a meal for Gilbert and her parents. But her mother had fainted straight away once she'd tried the food, her father had bolted for the toilet, and though Gilbert had cleaned his plate, he'd been laid up in bed all the next day.

She'd felt awful about it, recognizing that she'd really done something terrible. And she hadn't done any cooking at all ever since.

"But I mean, I can probably handle chopping potatoes..."

"You'll ruin the knife or the cutting board before you finish," insisted Oscar, not looking like he planned to give her back either item. "And how did you get hurt here anyway?"

When Oscar brushed a finger along her cheek, a tingling pain shot through it, causing her to wince. "Ouch!"

"That hurt?"

"Kinda..."

She'd felt considerable discomfort when he'd brushed her cheek. A splinter must have gotten lodged in there.

A vein throbbing in his temple, Oscar grabbed Cecilia's wrist in a viselike grip. "Come on, let's go."

As Oscar dragged her along, she protested, "Huh? Go where?"

"The first aid tent," he spat back, a sour look on his face.

"Here, look up. I'll disinfect the wound. Also, I think you have a splinter, so I'm going to take it out," announced Oscar, facing Cecilia in the empty first aid tent. With practiced motions, he took out tweezers, antiseptic, and gauze from the first aid kit and prepared to administer treatment.

Cecilia was frightened. "Y-you can do first aid?"

"I've got more knowledge and experience with it than you, I bet. Here, let me see," he ordered, grabbing her chin, tweezers in hand. As he tipped her head up to get a better look at the wound, Cecilia was completely flustered internally. It was the first time a boy had taken her chin and tilted her head up. At first glimpse, it looked like they were about to kiss.

"Hey—"

"Don't move," he implored as the tip of the tweezers touched her cheek. She wanted to pull back from the cold sensation, but Oscar wrapped a hand around the back of her neck this time, holding her in place. "I told you not to move."

"Sorry, it's just cold."

A serious expression on his face, Oscar fiddled with the tweezers over and over. The splinter seemed to be playing hard to get. After a dozen tries, she felt some discomfort and a dull pain in her cheek. "Ngh!"

"Stay still. I'm getting it out now."

A stinging pain followed the sensation of something being pulled from her cheek.

"There, I got it," Oscar announced, holding up a tiny splinter proudly.

"Thanks. You've got a steady hand, huh?" Cecilia replied.

"Steadier than yours," he retorted.

He was going to disinfect it next. Releasing her neck, he started readying a round cotton ball and antiseptic. "Okay. Look at me."

"Go ahead," she replied, facing him as directed. While she hated the sting of antiseptic, she knew she had to just accept her fate.

But even though she'd steeled herself for it, Oscar froze with a disinfectant-soaked cotton ball in hand. For several moments, he simply stared at her face.

"Uhhh…," she mumbled, making an impatient noise. She had

no idea why he was staring. What happened to cleaning the wound? "Are you not gonna…?"

"You're a guy, right?" Oscar blurted out, and Cecilia's heart leaped into her throat.

"H-heck yeah! I'm all man!" she cried, so shaken that her phrasing sounded unnatural, especially for her.

"Sure, yeah… Has anyone ever told you that you've got a girlie face?"

"I—I guess…," she replied. Of course, she couldn't claim that it wasn't a girlie face—it *was* a girl's face.

"It's because your eyelashes are long, and you don't have a strong jawline. Doesn't look like it's only because you don't work out enough. Sad, really," Oscar noted. It didn't sound like he suspected anything—he just pitied Cecil for his girlie mug.

He applied more antiseptic to the cotton ball and swabbed it along her cheek. A distinctive alcoholic scent wafted into the air, burning her nostrils. The liquid smarted on her skin, and pain lanced through that side of her face. "Ouch…"

"Little injuries like this do tend to hurt."

"Yeah, like when you get a paper cut."

"I hate that, too…," he admitted with a chuckle. Cecilia felt a little touched that she and Oscar were having a normal conversation.

Just like we're friends!

He could be a bit domineering and ridiculous, but this humanizing moment made her think he might actually be a regular person.

"I didn't expect you to be so well versed in first aid. I thought princes wouldn't know how," she admitted.

"It's because I've been instructed in swordplay since I was young. That's when I learned how to do simple first aid and resuscitation. I've actually ended up using those skills a lot," he explained.

"Huh. Do you find your training pretty difficult?"

"Mmm…it's normal."

"Normal?"

"It's like second nature to me," he said curtly, tossing the cotton ball in the trash.

"Like second nature," huh? Right, Oscar's Sacred Artifact is a sword. I guess that's why.

The Sacred Artifacts given to the knights were imbued with all sorts of powers. The full array of specialty offensive powers that could manifest included increased strength, basic clairvoyance, and healing of any wound, as well as Oscar's ability to slice through anything.

These powers stayed with the knights even if they gave their Sacred Artifact to a Holy Maiden candidate, so Gilbert—who'd given his to Cecilia—now had a power he could use if he wanted.

"Hmm?" she murmured, sensing someone close by. It was only for a moment, but she felt someone's piercing gaze on her from behind. But when she looked all around, no one was there. It was nothing.

"What's wrong?" Oscar asked.

"Nothing; just now I kinda…" She trailed off vaguely. There wasn't anyone or anything there, so there was no point calling attention to it.

I guess it was just my imagination?

The treatment apparently still underway, Oscar produced some medical tape from inside the first aid kit. As he cut it into strips the size of the wound, he asked falteringly, "How is…Cecilia?"

"Huh? O-oh, yeah. She's fine."

"Okay. That's good, then," Oscar replied, using the tape to cover the wound with gauze, presumably so dirt couldn't get in.

"Umm, why do you want to see Cecilia?" she asked, lulled by the easy atmosphere between them into asking the one thing she'd wanted to know for a while now.

"Why?"

In the game, Oscar wasn't this attached to Cecilia. Quite the opposite—forget being near her; he didn't want to even look at her. So why, then, did this Oscar want to see her and seem worried about how she was doing?

Maybe he's worried because without her around, he doesn't know what she's going to get up to?

People *did* fear invisible enemies—that much was true. Perhaps he felt uneasy, wondering if Cecilia was going to drive a wedge between him and Lean.

"I don't think Cecilia's going to get in your way. You'll never have to see her again if you don't want to!" she said.

"Never see her again? Did she say that?" he asked miserably, his voice so low it could sink into the ground. She'd said that as Cecilia with the best of intentions, but it evidently displeased him considerably.

"Umm…"

"Have I done something to her?"

"Huh?"

"I met her twelve years ago. Have I done something to hurt her feelings in that time? Is that why she's avoiding me?" Oscar asked, his gaze downcast and somewhat lonesome.

His expression surprised her so much that she flinched.

"I didn't mean to make her dislike me. I don't remember doing anything to upset her. So if you must know, one reason I'd like to meet her face-to-face is to ask her about that. And the other…"

"The other?"

"Is that I'd like to rebuild our relationship, if we can."

"What?!" she yelped, completely caught off guard. She could never have imagined he'd say that.

Rebuild our relationship? Does he mean that he wants us to be on good terms so he can marry Lean? He wants us to end our engagement amicably?

True; from Oscar's perspective, Cecilia's status as a daughter of House Sylvie posed a problem. He wanted to dissolve his engagement with her, but from a political standpoint, he couldn't sow discord with the Sylvies. Her parents were pleased with the match and might be distraught once they learned he'd called off the engagement only to choose a girl from a baron's house.

Maybe he wants to get me on his side to keep my parents in check!

From that angle, his obsession with Cecilia made more sense.

"S-so you don't hate her?" she asked nervously.

"How would I hate someone I haven't seen in twelve years? It's more like—"

"I see!" she interjected brightly, cutting Oscar off mid-sentence. "Got it! I understand now!"

Grinning widely, she clapped Oscar's shoulder firmly.

He didn't hate Cecilia. That was incomparably good news.

Now I might be able to escape my ruinous fate!

At the very least, he was no longer the man who wanted her dead.

She went on cheerfully, "Don't worry at all! Cecilia doesn't hate you! There's just a reason why she can't see anyone at the moment!"

"What do you mean? What reason?"

"It's...a secret?"

"Hey," Oscar growled, his voice lowering by another octave. However, his prickly aura had disappeared now that he'd revealed he didn't hate her.

"It's fine! You'll be able to meet with her when the time is right!" she crowed, pressing a fist to her chest.

When he broke off the engagement, she'd pop in to wish him well. She was, after all, brimming with happiness for him. He was a man in love.

Now I kinda want to cheer Oscar on!

Lean was on Jade's route right now, but that didn't mean she couldn't switch to Oscar. Depending on her efforts, his route was still very much in the cards for her.

"Oscar! You can do it! I'll support you any way I can!" she cried, clasping his hand in hers.

"Wha—?"

"Thanks! I'm so glad we talked!" she enthused, giving his hand a squeeze.

Just then, some female students' voices floated over. "Prince Cecil! Where are you?"

"Oh, do you need me? All right! I'm coming!" she shouted back, dropping his hand and leaping to her feet. She beamed her most radiant smile yet at him. "Let's both do our best, Oscar!"

She trotted out of the tent.

Oscar was left all alone in the first aid tent, wearing a dazed look with his cheeks flushed red.

"What's with that guy...?"

Even though there was no one around to see, he brought a hand up over his mouth, hiding his face.

"Why do my cheeks feel hot...?"

"I feel like someone's watching me...," Cecilia said, lying on her back and staring up at the ceiling from the top bunk she'd been assigned. Her thoughts were racing.

Ever since she and Oscar had gone to the first aid tent, she'd kept sensing someone's eyes on her. Initially, she'd dismissed it as her imagination, but feeling the penetrating gaze again at dinnertime was enough to convince her that someone was observing her.

"Who is it...?"

There had been too many people at dinner, so it had been impossible to pinpoint who it was. She sat up and looked down at her roommate, who was getting ready to head for the communal baths. "Hey, Oscar?"

"What?" he replied, turning back with a dark look. Maybe he didn't want anyone talking to him right now.

Paying him no mind, she continued. "I kinda feel like someone's watching me..."

"Well, it isn't me!" he shouted immediately. Cecilia was stunned. Why did it look like he was blushing?

"I know," she replied.

"O-okay...," he snapped, averting his gaze and stuffing his towel violently into his bag.

"Did you notice anyone staring at me? Especially at dinner. You were sitting next to me, right?"

"No, I didn't..."

"Huh, okay."

Maybe it's the Killer targeting me?

No one could establish the Killer's motive, but it was clear that they were trying to kill the potential Holy Maidens.

While the Killer hadn't yet claimed their first victim in this world, she couldn't rule out the possibility that after missing their chance to murder the azalea Holy Maiden, they'd seen through her cross-dressing disguise immediately and had come to snuff out her life.

There's no event like that in the game, but everything up until now has gone off the rails, so I can't be certain...

Maybe the third potential Holy Maiden had already been slain, and the papers just hadn't reported on it.

Now a little freaked out, Cecilia climbed down the stairs and went over to Oscar. He didn't turn around but said, "Anyway, aren't you gonna take a bath? If you don't get in there now, the communal baths will fill up."

"Oscar, you're actually pretty in touch with commoners," she commented.

"Huh?" he blurted out, looking back with a confused expression.

"I thought princes wouldn't go to communal baths," she explained.

And in the game, Oscar doesn't even go on the school camping trip in the first place.

"When would I ever have the chance except for right now?" he countered.

"Well, I guess that's true, since we're all nobility."

Few in aristocratic society learned about outdoor skills. Cooking, cleanup, communal bathing—all that was for the peasantry.

Although I personally love bathing with everyone in big, spacious baths.

But considering her current situation, that would be impossible. "I have to pass! I'm gonna use the shower in the room!"

"All right."

"Oh, wait, did you want us to go use the baths together?" she asked. Maybe Oscar was the type to enjoy *naked bonding.* She meant nothing else by it, but he went into a coughing fit as soon as he heard her.

"N-n-no! Of course not!"

"You don't have to reject it so strongly..."

"First of all, I have Cecilia! I'm not gonna... Not for you...," he babbled.

Why is this becoming about me personally?

He was now as red as a lobster and practically trembling. She didn't really understand what he was even getting at.

"I'm gonna go now...," he muttered, looking worn down. Cecilia nodded.

Just then, an unnatural *bang* sounded outside the window.

"What was that?!" she yelped, whirling around only to lock eyes with a black figure staring at her. They glared at Cecilia with bloodshot eyes.

"AAAAHHHHHH!" she shrieked, the blood draining from her face as she launched herself at Oscar, grabbing him around the waist in a tackle.

"Wha—?"

The force of her strike knocked his head back against the door. A sickening *crack* rang out in the room.

"Hey! What the hell, Cecil?!"

"O-Oscar! Th-there was someone peeping into the room just now!" she stammered, pointing at the window, still clutching his waist.

"What? Where? No one's there."

"Huh?"

Fearfully, she turned to glance back. Just as Oscar said, no one was there. "But... Wait, what? They're gone?"

"And this is the third floor anyway. How would anyone even climb up?" he pointed out.

Cecilia threw open the window and looked out. It was difficult to make out anything in the darkness, but from what she could see, no one was there.

"But I saw it...," she insisted in a forlorn voice. Oscar must have taken pity on her because he came out to inspect the area outside the window, too. Then he started.

"Hey, Cecil."

"What?"

"No matter how ridiculous you are, you haven't been leaving and entering through the window, right?"

"Of course not."

"Check this out," Oscar noted, pointing to the ledge below the window.

"What in the...?"

There was an unbelievably clear set of footprints.

Oh no... I can't sleep...

Eyes shut tight, Cecilia tossed and turned atop the bunk bed in her darkened room. She couldn't stop thinking about those footprints. Whenever she remembered the intense gaze of the person outside the window, she shivered.

I have to get some rest, though...

She squeezed her eyes shut even tighter. But sleep wouldn't come.

"You okay?"

A voice suddenly floated up from below, and Cecilia jumped. It was Oscar, who should have been fast asleep. "Can't sleep?"

"Kinda...," she answered, downplaying the truth.

"I didn't expect you to be such a scaredy-cat."

"Scaredy-cat...?"

"Considering how you're always rattling off those embarrassing lines so smoothly, I'd have thought you'd have more guts than this," Oscar teased, referring to when Cecil spoke to female students.

Cecilia pulled the covers up to her nose. "That's me working to sound manly, and it's not easy for me, either..."

"That's supposed to be manly?"

"Isn't it?"

"......"

Oscar's silence was pointed, his reaction similar to Gil's earlier. Evidently, there was a big gap between what she thought was manly and what they considered manly.

"So you're telling me you force yourself to act that way toward the girls?"

"I'm not forcing myself. I like girls! But I guess it's true that it gets exhausting."

"I guess you've suffered in your own way with that feminine face of yours...," Oscar acknowledged.

At some point, her dread had dissipated. Their conversation must have diverted it. But she hadn't noticed and so chatted happily with him about silly things for a while longer. As the conversation went on, Oscar's voice began to grow tired.

"Oscar, are you sleepy?"

"Mmm," he mumbled. She could tell he was rubbing his eyes from the rustling of the covers.

Cecilia didn't want him to sleep, personally, but he needed to. "Sorry for keeping you up. Let's go to sleep."

"...'m still okay," he protested.

"Then why do you sound like you could fall asleep at any minute?" she teased wryly, then added, "Good night."

Oscar bade good night to her, too.

The room fell into silence, only for the same terror to come creeping back up from her toes.

Who was the Killer? Why hadn't they murdered the azalea Holy Maiden this time around? Who was peering in at her from the window?

What if they really are targeting me?

Once it grew quiet, doubt filled her mind once again. Up until now, she'd thought things would somehow work out in the end. In fact, since no one had gotten killed, she'd happily assumed that she and Lean would also remain unharmed. But now that it had come to this, she realized how naive that train of thought had been. No wonder Gil had gotten mad at her.

The chills of fright running down her spine were keeping her wide awake. At this rate, she was going to pull an unintentional, unwanted all-nighter.

"Cecil," came a voice from below.

Cecilia's eyes shot open. "Oscar, you're still up?"

"If you're still scared, do you want to sleep down here with me?" he asked innocently.

"Huh?" she squeaked, out of shock. Naturally, she hadn't anticipated that option.

"You don't have to if you don't want to..."

"Umm...," she answered, considering his offer. The mattresses in the bunk beds weren't too narrow for two people to sleep on. She would actually have to stretch out both arms all the way to just barely touch both sides of the bed. It wouldn't exactly be roomy, but they wouldn't be jammed together, either.

The issue was that she had to drift off with her wig on, but since not being able to sleep was a more pressing concern, she didn't linger on that detail.

It would be improper for an unmarried boy and girl to share a bed, but right now she was Cecil, a man. Two boys could share a bed without a problem. Probably...

I do think I might be able to sleep if I'm with someone...

Plucking up her courage, she said, "Okay then, can I?"

"Sure."

"It's really okay?"

"Stop questioning it," he insisted dryly.

After fixing her wig, she grabbed her blanket and pillow and went down the ladder. When she pulled back the curtain and looked inside the bottom bunk, she saw that Oscar had already moved over closer to the wall for her. *This guy actually said yes* was written all over his face. Still, he wasn't acting displeased, which was very considerate of him.

"Excuse me," she said, crawling in. The bed was still a little warm from Oscar's body heat, so once she added the blanket she'd brought down, it was nice and toasty.

So warm...

She felt a little touched. "Thanks, Oscar."

"Sure. I don't blame you after what happened," he responded. He was sticking as close to the wall as possible.

"You can wake me up if I snore too loud."

"You snore?"

She giggled. "Whenever I sneak into Gil's bed, he always kicks me out because of it."

"You two sure are close," Oscar replied, sounding a bit put off.

"That's because we've known each other since we were young."

"So you're like brothers?"

"Yup. Like brothers...siblings..."

As they kept on rambling about everything and nothing, she suddenly started to feel hazy. She was getting sleepy. "Oscar...I'm..."

"Go to sleep."

"Okay," she answered, lying with her back to him and shutting her eyes. She was asleep in seconds.

"What the...? He doesn't snore at all," Oscar whispered after making sure Cecil was unconscious. The other boy had gone out like a light so quickly it made Oscar suspect he'd been lying about being unable to drift off.

He snoozed soundly, a look of peace on his face.

Sneaking close, Oscar brushed aside a lock of hair to look at Cecil's face. That was a girl's face through and through. Him being a boy was the real shock.

"His face really is so feminine. And he's so thin..."

When the Obstruction had first appeared in the auditorium, Cecil had moved in such a way that one could clearly see his muscles. And yet, his body was still so slender despite that, with a waist so slim one could mistake it for a woman's.

"What if he's actually a girl…? No, that can't be true, can it?"

If that were the case, he wouldn't have crawled into another boy's bed so nonchalantly.

"Although, I do feel like I've seen his face somewhere…"

Oscar scrutinized every inch of Cecil's face but couldn't think of anyone who fit that description.

"Nngh!" the other boy groaned in a low voice, turning over in his sleep. Perhaps he'd felt Oscar's gaze on him. When he did, his nose brushed against Oscar's, who had come close to examine him.

Whoa!

Oscar frantically scooted back; they'd been close enough to kiss. He plastered himself against the wall to put distance between them, his heart pounding out of his chest. When he clapped a hand over his face, it felt so flushed that he knew without looking in a mirror how red his cheeks must be.

"No, no, no! I was just surprised! He's a guy, and I'm a guy!" he reminded himself.

He knew the name of this feeling. But if he deigned to name it, there would be no going back.

"I have Cecilia."

His first love floated to mind. The girl in his memories had made his stomach swoop and his heart flutter, exactly as the boy before him did now.

"Dammit. I shouldn't have let myself go there…," he muttered, displeased with his abundantly clear train of thought.

The next day's schedule called for courses on orienteering and navigation.

This consisted of going around a hiking trail in the forest and collecting stamps from various points. It was closer to an extended walk than a hike in terms of difficulty, so the noble-born Vleugel Academy students enjoyed getting all the stamps.

Among them was a boy of ashen countenance.

Cecil Admina—or rather, Cecilia.

I didn't foresee this turn of events...

As she climbed up a gently sloping trail, she gazed at the sky beseechingly. The source of her anxiety was the individual who'd peeped into her room the night before.

We told the teachers, but the footprints are gone. What do I do now...?

Soon after discovering the tracks, Oscar had gone to report the situation to the faculty member closest to their room, Mordred. But when Mordred returned to the room to see it for himself, the marks had already disappeared.

Only a few minutes had passed since Oscar and Cecilia had discovered them.

Those footprints were so distinct, and yet they were wiped clean without a trace. Did someone rub them away? But I didn't notice anyone there...

If someone *had* cleared them away, that meant they had to have been there on the other side. But that seemed impossible. Both Cecilia and Oscar had checked outside the window. She could only conclude that the wind had blown them away.

But it wasn't that windy last night...

That ledge outside the window ran all around the building.

Whoever did it could have left their room and crept along the ledge to reach Cecilia and Oscar's.

She had to do something if it turned out that her Peeping Tom was the Killer.

"Haaaaaaahhh…"

As she brooded, someone let out a ridiculous-sounding yawn next to her. She looked over to find Oscar rubbing his eyes.

"Oscar, you look exhausted. You couldn't sleep last night?"

After a pregnant pause, he admitted, "Yeah."

Cecilia cocked her head. "Was I snoring too loud?"

"No… But anyway, I just had a conversation with Dr. Mordred. He said that at this stage, there's nothing we can do yet. He did inform the other teachers about it at the staff meeting, at least…"

It was obvious that Oscar had changed the subject, but she didn't question it too deeply, simply answering, "Huh, okay."

I bet it was *my snoring…*

Her face reddened. Noisy snoring was disgraceful and unbecoming of a proper young lady. She may be a man right now, true, but that didn't matter.

Based on the way Oscar was helping her, he seemed to be taking the matter seriously as well. She welcomed any and all allies, gratefully accepting his goodwill.

"Anyway, do you have any idea who was at the window?" he asked.

"Nope, not a clue." She sighed, shaking her head. The truth was that she did, but he wouldn't believe her if she told him, on top of inviting needless suspicion.

And besides, she didn't particularly want to tell anyone other than Gilbert about her past life.

"What about you, Oscar? Do you have any guesses?"

"No, I don't, either… If Dante had come on this trip, I would have thought maybe it was him pulling a dumb prank, but he's not here…"

Dante was Oscar's friend and one of the love interests. He was a troublemaker with a bit of a record; she truly respected the prince for maintaining a friendship with him.

"Ooh, I see," Cecilia replied.

"At the very least, I hope this is all just a joke."

"Right," she answered, which was just when she sensed someone behind her. She whirled around to see Lean standing there with a sweet smile.

"What have the two of you been whispering about?" Lean asked.

"Lean! Oh, um..."

"You must be really close!" she continued.

"Does it look that way?" Oscar responded, lifting an eyebrow. For some odd reason, he seemed pleased about this.

Still smiling sweetly, Lean fell into step with them. "If there's anything bothering you, will you let me in on it, too? I'd love to be of help to the both of you."

"I suppose."

"Well...," Cecilia trailed off, dropping her gaze. True, it would be helpful to have more people in her corner. But if that really was the Killer, telling Lean could make her a target, too, since she was a potential Holy Maiden. She didn't want to put Lean at risk.

Moreover, the protagonist had a very important date that night—her infamous event with Jade. Cecilia's own future hinged on this monumental occasion, which she couldn't afford to ruin by fussing over a voyeur.

Cecilia squeezed Lean's shoulder. "You can't. I won't get you involved in this."

"But—"

"This is our problem to solve. I don't want to put you in danger," Cecilia insisted, the usual princely smile plastered onto her face. In response, it was not Lean but the girls around them who let out squeals. Some were even so moved and excited that they fainted.

"So, in other words, you don't want me intruding on your little secret?"

"I…guess so," Cecilia replied. Since the ogler had targeted her and Oscar's room, it was fair to say that it was their *little secret.* Lean wasn't wrong, although her phrasing made Cecilia a little uncomfortable.

"In that case, I shouldn't be interfering with your secret. If anything happens, you can call on me anytime and I'll do whatever I can!" Lean announced, flashing a smile so bright it chased away any discomfort, before curtsying to them. Even Cecilia had to admit her adorable smile was practically angelic. Lean really was the embodiment of love.

With that, she left them and ran over to Jade, who appeared to have been pining for her return. Reunited, they began chatting animatedly with each other.

Those two really are so close… But aren't they not supposed to be this public with their affections yet?

Around this time in the game, Lean is still too self-conscious to get close to Jade in public. But they were already carrying on so affectionately, without a care in the world for who might see.

I guess this part of the story has gotten a little off track, too?

It could be another element that deviated from the game, like how Gilbert hadn't grown up dour and gloomy and how Oscar was much friendlier. Cecilia mused on that as she watched them.

"So what are you thinking of for tonight? You want to catch the Peeping Tom?" Oscar proposed, bringing her back to reality. She'd thought he'd be upset to see his crush Lean so close with another guy, but that wasn't the case at all. He was acting perfectly natural, no different than usual. What an unexpectedly open-minded man.

Cecilia nodded. "Yep, that's the plan."

"But how should we catch them? We don't even know what they look like…"

"I have an idea!" she cried. He glanced down at her with surprise. In response, she confidently clasped a hand to her chest. "I'm going to be a decoy!"

At night after dinner, Cecilia crept into the woods alone and lingered in an area on the stamp-collecting hiking trail. The place was so open that it was practically deserted, with good visibility to boot. It was also the perfect distance from the lodge, just far enough so that she wouldn't interrupt Lean and Jade on their date event. She'd had her eyes on this spot since passing it earlier in the day.

She planted her hands on her hips and waited.

If this really is the Killer we're up against, they'll be looking to strike when I'm alone!

Of course, she didn't intend to just present her head on a platter, so Oscar was watching from a distance.

The plan was simple. Cecilia would act as a decoy and await the Killer by herself. When the assailant struck, the two of them would subdue them. The Killer of the game is a single individual, so Oscar and Cecilia should be able to capture them together. The plan hinged on that condition.

Additionally, the Killer never attacks the knights voluntarily in the game, so they wouldn't search for Oscar instead, who was currently hidden.

I actually wanted to watch the event to make sure it goes well, but considering the circumstances, my hands are tied.

As far as she could tell, Lean and Jade were totally in love. Something was bound to happen between them regardless of whether Cecilia was watching or not. In fact, she might have actually gotten in their way if she did attend.

Determined, Cecilia huffed defiantly. "Come at me anytime! I'm gonna see who you really are!"

But despite her enthusiasm, no one ever appeared, even after a lengthy wait. Nor did she sense that piercing, intense gaze on her.

The sound of the wind rustling the leaves was the only thing echoing through the woods.

"I guess maybe it was all in my head…"

Cecilia sighed in disappointment after biding her time for an hour with nothing to show for it. She hadn't *wanted* anyone to pop up, but it nevertheless felt like a bit of a letdown that no one had revealed themselves.

"I guess they're not coming tonight?" Oscar conceded, appearing from deep within the forest, visibly impatient. As he cracked his neck, he explained, "I got tired of waiting."

"Sorry. I guess nothing's going to happen…"

"In this instance, it's good that your fears turned out to be groundless. No need to apologize," Oscar consoled, his voice gentle.

Head hung in dejection, Cecilia said, "You're so nice, Oscar. Thank you."

As a smile split her face, Oscar's cheeks reddened just a little. "N-no, I'm not! I'm not being nice to you specifically! I'd be nice to anyone!"

"Are you sure you should be saying that about yourself?"

"Shut up!" Oscar retorted, his lips pursed in embarrassment.

He's gotten a lot cuter somehow.

Until very recently, Oscar had been the kind of person she didn't care for, but their time on the school camping trip had deepened her understanding of him.

Just then, a metallic rattling sounded. Someone had tripped the makeshift alarm of empty cans tied together with string that Cecilia had strung up around the vicinity before lying in wait for the voyeur.

"Where's that coming from?!" Oscar shouted, anxious at the clear sign that someone had arrived. Then something rustled in the low bushes behind them.

"There!" he cried, grabbing his Sacred Artifact. The silver bangle instantly changed shape and mass, morphing into a sword.

"Wow!" Cecilia gasped, awestruck at her first glimpse of a Sacred Artifact transforming. The game never showed that.

He hurled the sword forward, and it flew straight on without getting lodged in any of the trees.

His Sacred Artifact was endowed with the ability to slice through anything. Wood, metal, diamonds—all were like butter in the face of his blade. On top of that, it would not cut through anything the wielder did not wish to disturb.

This meant his flying brand would not nick or graze any of the trees—it would only stab into its target.

"AAAHHHH!" someone screamed. They followed the sound only to encounter two entirely unexpected individuals—Lean and Jade.

Oscar's sword was stuck fast in the tree next to them, but the blade was missing half its length—no, it only *appeared* that way.

The sword had pierced Jade's Sacred Artifact, which specialized in concealment. Simply laying that cloak over someone or something would grant them invisibility and render their presence undetectable. His cloak was draped over the sword blade, concealing half of it from sight.

Oscar and Cecilia approached the pair, who were sprawled on the ground.

"What are you two doing here?" asked Cecilia.

"Are you responsible for all this?" demanded Oscar.

"Ah-ha-ha..."

Huddling together, Lean and Jade let out strained laughs.

"Why?!" Cecilia cried, about to press them for answers.

But before they could respond, a scream rose up from the direction of the lodge. The four of them rushed over to find a flood of students pouring out the doors.

Behind them, a wild-eyed student and several stray dogs were going on a rampage.

"Ah, Obstructions," Oscar observed calmly.

Cecilia's eyes widened. This was Jade and Lean's event.

"Forget about all that back there for now. We have to save everyone!" Lean implored, agitated.

While Cecilia didn't consider that something to let slide even for a moment, Lean was right. The most important thing right now was preventing the Obstructions from causing any harm.

I'll help save them, but I'm not going to mess up any events this time!

She recalled that she'd ended up interfering during the prologue and during Oscar and Lean's first event. Cecilia had a bad habit of losing sight of everything around her when she panicked.

"Anyone who's injured, get over here!" shouted Mordred from behind. He was using his Sacred Artifact to heal the wounds of both students and teachers. His power was apt for a doctor.

A potential Holy Maiden who had yet to receive a Sacred Artifact was essentially powerless. All she could do was touch the mark on an Obstruction to exorcise it. However, if she did have Sacred Artifacts, she could draw on the respective powers they granted to her knights. Therefore, a candidate with multiple Artifacts in her possession would be stronger than any of her individual suitors.

By the same token, Cecilia could now use Gilbert's Artifact.

I think his had the power of...

"Cecil!" Oscar cried.

She shouldn't have gotten distracted trying to sift through her memories. If not for him, she wouldn't have noticed the wild dogs leaping at her from behind. She touched the Artifact.

"Aroo!"

With a spray of popping sparks, it repelled the beasts before they could even touch Cecilia, slamming them into the ground. A black mist rose up from their bodies and vanished.

Now I remember. Gil's Artifact...

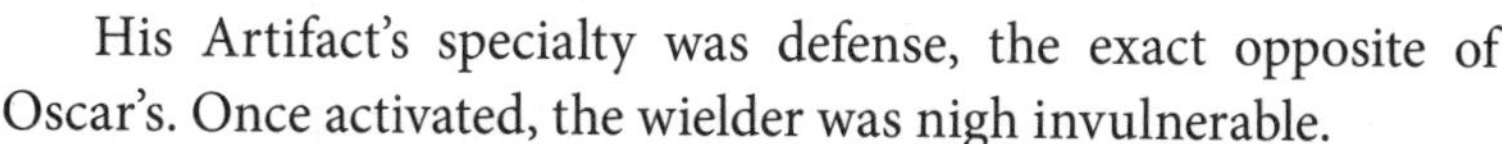

His Artifact's specialty was defense, the exact opposite of Oscar's. Once activated, the wielder was nigh invulnerable.

That means I can—

Cecilia drew close to him. "I'll help the rest of the students and teachers escape, so you handle the Obstructions. My Artifact isn't exactly made for exorcising them…"

"Sure, that works…"

"Jade, can you stick with Lean? And help Oscar out if you can," Cecilia continued.

"Got it," Jade said.

"Yes," Lean replied.

She wasn't going to forget about getting them together. Jade still needed to be wounded while protecting Lean.

Urgh, but this means I'm going to let him get hurt…

Beset by the pangs of her conscience, Cecilia clutched her chest. While she knew it was necessary and that he wouldn't be seriously injured, it still pained her.

But if she prevented this event from happening, a bleak future would await.

Even if Jade has to suffer, I at least want to keep it to a minimum! Oh…I know!

"Oscar!" she cried, tugging on his sleeve to stop him in his tracks on his way over to the lodge.

"…What?"

"Um, stay with Jade. Don't let him get too hurt…"

"Huh? Okay…"

"I know you can do it!" she reassured him, clutching his hand.

His face instantly pinkened. "Y-yeah, just trust in me!"

"I will. Do your best!"

"Sure," Oscar replied, awkwardly averting his eyes.

That should ensure Jade wouldn't get too banged up.

"All right! I'm gonna do my best, too!" Cecilia shouted enthusiastically, hyping herself up. She had a mission of her own to accomplish. Although this was an event from the game's narrative, she wanted to protect as many people as possible.

She touched the bracelet and burst into the lodge as screams filled her ears.

About a half hour later, the situation showed signs of being under control. Most of the Obstructions had vanished, and the students and teachers were scattered around outside the lodge, watching.

As soon as Cecilia emerged with the last person in tow, Jade, Lean, and Oscar followed. They must have finished exorcising the Obstructions.

Lean spotted Cecilia and ran over, frowning in worry. "Lord Cecil, are you all right?"

"Yes. Thank you, I'm fine," Cecilia reassured, smiling at Lean, who seemed to have been concerned about Cecil's solo mission.

Oscar followed after Lean. Mud spattered his cheeks. "Doesn't look like you got hurt."

"Um, same for...you," Cecilia said, looking over at Jade. He was the picture of health, not a scratch on him. She cocked her head. "Why isn't anyone injured?"

"You sound like you wanted us to get hurt," Oscar said.

"No, not *you*...," she replied, though there was no way she could follow it up with *I wanted Jade to get hurt*.

There was also the matter of how Jade and Lean had been observing Cecilia. This event felt strange somehow.

Then she heard a growl from behind. The second she turned around, something launched at her. Caught off guard, Cecilia landed flat on the ground. A black blur rushed straight for Lean.

"LEAN!"

"Eek!"

It was an Obstruction possessing a feral dog. Jade, who was closest, jumped in front of Lean. It looked exactly as the scene does in the game.

"Jade!"

But then someone who isn't in this scene at all cried out as a sword swung down at the assailant. It went through the canine's body without cutting any of its flesh, only rending the black fog clinging to it in half.

The animal collapsed, unconscious and inert. Its ears were still twitching, so it didn't appear to be dead.

"Phew. I guess we hadn't gotten them all…," Oscar remarked, shaking his sword like he was flicking blood off it before sheathing it.

Cecilia stared, stunned by what had just happened. "Why…?"

"Hmm?"

"Wh-why did you defeat it?!"

"Huh?" Oscar said, frowning in confusion. "It was an Obstruction. You're supposed to defeat them!"

"But, but—," Cecilia spluttered, her lips trembling querulously. Her fate had just been sealed right before her eyes.

It was good that Lean and Jade were both uninjured. Cecilia hadn't *wanted* them to get hurt, of course.

Still, though…

"But—," she protested again, though she couldn't say, *But the event!* like she was saying in her heart.

"You're the one who just told me you knew I could do it, so what's going on?" he demanded.

"Prince Oscar has been in very high spirits ever since you said that!" Lean informed Cecilia.

"No, I haven't!" Oscar denied. His face reddened, possibly from happiness, and he jerked his head aside.

Cecilia thought back to their exchange from earlier.

"Um, stay with Jade. Don't let him get too hurt…"

"Huh? Okay…"

"I know you can do it!"

She was flummoxed. *What I said affected him that much?!*

Her heart flipped in her chest as mortification, regret, and anger at herself warred with one another.

Glaring at the ground, she let out a little groan of frustration. Then she noticed a notebook lying at her feet. "What's this?"

Thinking nothing of it, she picked it up and flipped through its contents.

And yet, what she found inside was…

Cecil held Oscar locked inside his willowy arms.

Delirious from the heat of the aphrodisiac, Oscar was unable to put up anything more than a token resistance. He gazed up at Cecil, eyes glazed over.

The other boy smirked, his grin suggestive and utterly enchanting. "Don't try to fight it, Oscar."

Then Cecil pressed him flat on his back…

"AAAAAHHHHH!" Cecilia shrieked, slamming the notebook shut.

It turned out it was illicit smut of *that* nature. Not only that, but she and Oscar were the stars!

And I'm the one on top?!

"Ce-Cecil! Hey! That's mine! It's really embarrassing—don't look!" cried Jade, *of all people*, snatching it back. His cheeks were flushed with humiliation as he asked, "Did you see?"

When Cecilia nodded, he moaned in despair and fidgeted nervously.

Apparently, Jade was the true main character of the dating sim, what with him carrying on like some blushing maiden.

Red in the face, he confessed, "So actually, we've been writing fanfic about you two…"

"…Fanfic?" she repeated.

"Lean also draws art of you."

"*Tasteful* art, thank you," emphasized Lean, also blushing.

Cecilia felt a headache building. "Hold on—can I just confirm something? Why have the two of you been passing this notebook around?"

"We use it to write our fics," Jade answered.

"So you two were the ones spying on me earlier?" Cecilia pressed.

"We were gathering material!" Lean announced proudly.

Cecilia was about to have a nervous breakdown from being pummeled with these revelations. And Jade had even used his Artifact to spy on her for more material. They could both stand to be a lot less audacious.

"Cecil, I'm sorry. But it's because Gilbert/Cecil is my OTP!" yelled Jade.

"What exactly are you apologizing for…?" asked Cecilia. Her complexion had turned unintentionally stony. She covered her eyes, pitying her brother for getting dragged into all this.

"Then I have to state that *my* preference is for Cecil/Gilbert!" Lean cut in. "Of course, my all-time favorite pairing is Cecil/Oscar because of how it emphasizes Lord Cecil's dark side, but if you want to talk Lord Gilbert pairings, Cecil/Gilbert is *right* there! As far as I'm concerned, Lord Cecil will always be the top, now and forever!"

"I'm not the top *or* the bottom!" Cecilia protested.

"I'm not going to accept either of them as verse. I've always thought they're too out of character when Lean tries that, " Jade argued.

"We're right here! Don't talk about in or out of character!" Cecilia interjected with exasperation, but even pointing that out to them did little to stem the tide of their heated debate.

Incidentally, Oscar was standing off to the side, wearing a look of befuddlement, unable to follow their argument at all.

"Can I ask one final question?" Cecilia requested.

"Yes, what is it?" replied Lean.

"What?" asked Jade.

Cecilia took a deep breath. "What are the two of you to each other?"

"Friends who share the same interests!" declared Lean.

"Friends who share the same creative spirit!" announced Jade at the same time.

Cecilia practically died on the spot.

✦ CHAPTER 4 ✦ Duel of the Siblings

Nearly one week after returning from their outdoor education course...

"Hey, Gil."

"Yes?"

"C'mon, don't be like that..."

"I'm the same as ever," Gilbert sniffed.

His mood was at an all-time low. Cecilia frowned, inspecting him as they strolled together from the dorms to the academy.

He'd been in a real funk lately. Though he would answer if she spoke to him and eat lunch with her if she asked, his responses were even more clipped than usual.

They hadn't had a fight. Something else must have been bothering him.

I bet that's it...

Cecilia eyed some female students squealing together on a bench. They were holding a book.

"Here it is, the famous Madame Neal's novel! My friend finally lent it to me!"

"This is the one with the guys who really sound like Prince Cecil and Prince Oscar, right? Ooh, I've wanted to read it for so long!"

"Carol said she cried reading it. Her eyes were all red this morning!"

"I really can't wait!"

As they glowed with happiness, the two girls' eyes fluttered shut, and they fell into a reverie. Cecilia felt her cheeks growing gaunt with exhaustion just watching them.

Recently, Lean's...*story* had somehow gotten popular among the students. Apparently, she'd printed several copies of it herself and left them lying around the school library. Her coconspirator in printing the books was Jade, of course, who'd gotten involved with the printing business of late.

Merely three days later, all the female students had fallen in love with their creation.

Incidentally, the author's pen name, Neal, was an anagram of Lean.

When the book first started to spread, Cecilia asked to meet with Lean to understand why she was doing this. According to her, it was because she wanted to make more friends who shared her... interests.

Even though she'd successfully lured Jade into her web, evidently, he alone was not enough. Dragging people down into hell with her, Lean explained proudly, meant exposing them to stories that would resonate with them.

"My greatest concern at the moment is that I am the only creator of this content. Therefore, I'm going to train up other authors from scratch!"

Lean's spirited tone reverberated again in her ear. This was one aggressive girl.

The reason behind Gilbert's foul mood had to be the story Lean had written.

"I'm surprised by how tolerant you are of all this, Cecil," Gilbert barked caustically, his mouth turned down in a sour moue.

He'd called her Cecil because they were in public. "Getting used for her filth and with His Highness to boot."

"It's not like it's anything explicit, and while the characters may be based on Oscar and me, the names are different. It isn't worth making a stink about..." Cecilia sighed.

Lean had indeed modeled her characters on Oscar and Cecil, but since she'd altered their names for publication, Cecilia had lost the right to complain. Lean could shut down any of her objections simply by insisting that they were original characters. Nevertheless, everyone could vaguely intuit who they were from their mannerisms and styles of talking.

"I disagree. Original novel or not, I don't like it one bit," Gilbert stated flatly. In other words, he didn't like seeing Oscar and Cecil flirting and kissing in the story. He glared at the text like it was dirt. "And what's worse is that you've *actually* gotten closer to His Highness..."

His voice dropped even lower. He seemed quite perturbed that Oscar and Cecil had developed an oddly friendly relationship ever since coming back from the school camping trip.

Cecilia scratched at her cheek, grinning sheepishly. "A lot happened on the trip. I learned that Oscar's not such a bad guy after all. Although I'll admit I was pretty worried when I found out we'd be sharing a room."

"Excuse me? Sharing a room?"

"Oops."

Gilbert eyes widened as he stared at her in complete and utter disbelief.

She broke out in a cold sweat. Since she'd known him for so long, she was well aware that she'd just hit a sore spot.

He stopped dead in his tracks before stomping right up to her. Trying to edge away from him, Cecilia ended up with her back pressed against the building.

"What does that mean, you shared a room? At the school camp? You didn't have single rooms?"

"Ah, um, well… We had to draw lots and then by coincidence…"

"Draw lots…?" Gilbert repeated, his face darkening by the second. He glowered at her with eyes as black as obsidian. And the scariest part was how his face was half covered by shadow.

She wrung her hands nervously. "Ah! But I didn't get caught! We did sleep in the same bed, but nothing happened!"

"The same…bed…?"

His expression went blank in an instant. At that moment, Cecilia learned firsthand how truly terrifying an expressionless face could be.

"Why? Did he pull you in against your will?" Gilbert demanded.

"Umm, well… A lot happened, and I got scared…"

"You got in his bed *voluntarily*?"

"It kinda ended up that way?" she squeaked before hearing Gilbert audibly grind his teeth in frustration. She braced herself for a scolding.

But it never came; he didn't yell or even raise his voice. Far from it—he turned aside and marched away. His strides were huge, like he wasn't waiting for Cecilia to catch up.

"Hey! Gil, wait up!"

"Sorry. I don't think I can look at you right now."

"Wh-why are you so mad?! This is different from your earlier funk, isn't it? Did I do something?" she called after him. He was so incensed that it made her panic.

He kept walking farther and farther away. She caught up and grabbed his arm to stop him, but he shook her off.

"Gil, please!"

"Leave me alone for a while. I'll cool off by the time I see you again," he barked, leaving her with that as he strode briskly into the school.

She watched him go with a tight expression on her face. "Yikes. I really pissed him off..."

Duke Coulson, a distant relative of the house of Duke Sylvie, had three sons.

The first two were terribly brilliant, so talented that either could inherit the title. Their parents doted on them, showering them with as much love as was humanly possible.

However, their youngest—Gilbert—had a rough upbringing and was often referred to as his brothers' watered-down knockoff.

He lived in a separate house from the rest of his family, and his parents only came to see him once a month. He yearned for his mother's affection and appealed to her for it countless times, but she never once indulged him. It was always up to the servants to care for and play with him.

They were his family, but they didn't act like it.

Such was Gilbert's place in House Coulson. Talk of him getting adopted into House Sylvie started right around when he began to completely despair about his life there.

At the time, Duke Sylvie was anxious because he had a five-year-old daughter but no male heir. Ancient tradition dictated that only men could inherit hereditary peerages. Exceptions were allowed for very unusual cases, but they were practically unheard of.

Nobles were duty bound to leave behind heirs and inheritors. Accordingly, Duke Sylvie selected the Coulsons to adopt from, as they had three sons.

At first, Gilbert's second eldest brother was going to leave. If things went well, he would inherit the Sylvie dukedom. However, the possibility remained that if the Sylvies had a son, the second eldest brother could get the cold shoulder. The duchess was still young and could very well get pregnant again.

Owing to that concern, House Coulson selected Gilbert, since it wouldn't matter if he was neglected.

The day he left for the Sylvie manor, not a single member of his family saw him off.

"Did they just abandon me?" Gilbert asked a servant.

The servant bowed deeply and told him, "Please have a safe journey."

The Sylvies had given Gilbert a warm welcome. In fact, they were overjoyed to have him.

His new adopted sister Cecilia was especially thrilled, crying out, "I finally have a little brother!" and hugging him.

Despite how she received him, Gilbert didn't like her at first.

That was an understatement: He loathed her. *Despised* her. As someone who couldn't inherit the family title, she was in the same position as him, yet *her* parents had adored and spoiled her. So strong was their love that she was almost drowning in it.

"Why are things so different even though our circumstances are the same?"

That thought plagued him after coming to live at Sylvie manor.

One day, after he'd been there about half a year, Gilbert fell ill. In addition to having a high fever, he was so fatigued that he couldn't get out of bed on his own for a while.

Gilbert's constitution was delicate by nature. That had been true at Coulson manor as well, and he was always getting sick. His parents didn't like that about him, so every time he came down with something, they'd let slip to the servants remarks like "*What a bother*" and "*Quite pathetic.*" He couldn't remember them ever showing concern for him.

"Gil, are you okay?"

Cecilia had come to check on him many times since he'd fallen ill. Sometimes it was to change the cool cloth on his forehead, while other times, it was to play nurse. Gilbert found it all so irritating he could hardly stand it. With how clumsy she was, she didn't make much of a nurse, so it seemed very much like simply an extension of playing house. She treated him like a doll.

When he thought about it in that way, it infuriated him.

But if he drove her out of his room then, he could lose his place in House Sylvie as well. So he resigned himself to swallowing his complaints and playing the role of her doll.

She never tired of it and came to visit every single day. She would sing lullabies and read books to him to her heart's content.

At the end, she always asked him if there was anything he wanted. He always shook his head no.

That day had been much the same.

After wiping his sweat away and reading books to him until her throat had gone dry, she croaked, "Do you want anything?"

Normally that was when he'd shake his head, but Gilbert was feeling a little different that day. He wanted to be a little mean to his hypocrite of a foster sister.

He pointed to an illustrated page in the book Cecilia had read to him. It was a picture of a blue rose said to be capable of granting any wish. "I want that," he answered.

Blue roses didn't exist. Gilbert had known that when he made his request. He wanted to see the distressed look on her face.

But after humming thoughtfully to herself as she looked at the picture, Cecilia cried, "I've got it! I'll find one by tomorrow!"

Though he was surprised, he let it go, reasoning that she was just unaware that blue roses didn't exist.

Sure enough, she didn't show up the next day around the time she always came. She must have been in a serious fix. Thinking about that improved his mood a lot. But he simultaneously felt lonely in his room, which was so much quieter than usual.

That night, Gilbert awoke to a tapping sound. When he sat up and looked around, he saw Cecilia at the window. Her cheeks were smeared with mud, and she was clutching something in one hand. He rushed to open the window, whereupon she presented him with a single flower.

"Sorry. This was the only blue flower I could find!" she told him, holding out a blue gentian. "Apparently, it can be made into medicine, too! It grows halfway up the cliff, so it was pretty hard to pick."

"The cliff?!" he yelped. Yes, there was a cliff behind the main estate, but surely she hadn't really climbed it all alone?

Upon closer inspection, her dress was dirty and its hem was torn, like it had gotten caught on something. Her face was lined with scratches, and a red lump sat on her forehead.

"I skipped out on my lessons today, so Mother will be ever so upset with me," she announced, grinning all the while.

Gilbert accepted the gentian with shaky hands. "Why…?"

His voice quivered, too. Why would she have gone to so much trouble? He couldn't understand.

"Because I love you, Gil! I've been so sad that you haven't been feeling well!" she declared honestly, beaming an innocent smile at him. Then she patted his head with one muddy hand. "Right? I hope we can play together soon!"

"Mmm…"

His eyes welled up. The tears fell and rolled down his cheeks. No one had ever told him they loved him in his entire life. This was the first time he learned how heartwarming those words could be.

"What's wrong, Gil? Does something hurt?" she fretted, peering closely at him from outside the window. Now he noticed that her honey-blond hair, usually beautifully combed, was all tangled. She must have tripped over and over.

Gilbert wiped his tears. "No, I'm just thinking that I love you, too, Sister."

"Oh!" she gasped, giving him the widest smile he'd seen from her yet.

From then on, Gilbert adored his new big sister. It didn't take him long to realize his feelings for her were romantic, and by the time he did, he was past the point of no return.

Cecilia still viewed him as her little brother. Since he understood that, he would never make any sort of move. And yet, neither could he give up on her, so he was steadily taking steps to remove obstacles from his way.

He'd already gotten permission from Cecilia's parents to propose should her engagement with the crown prince ever get called off. They were brother and sister on the family records, but that didn't mean it was impossible for them to marry.

"So then, why is some other random guy just strolling on in...?"

He didn't hate Oscar. But it was a different story with Cecilia involved.

Awful feelings filled his heart.

As if a black mist had risen from his tightly clasped hands.

The same day she'd upset Gilbert, Cecilia lunched in the dining hall. "What do I do...?"

Leaving her fork stabbed into the quiche that came with her meal, she fell prostrate onto the table. Normally, she would have lunch with Gilbert, but considering what had just happened that morning, she obviously couldn't invite him. And judging by how her brother hadn't sent out an invitation of his own, he probably didn't want to see her today.

Incidentally, the female students besotted with Prince Cecil no longer approached her indiscriminately, evidently due to some pact they had made among themselves. They still gazed at Cecil ardently, of course, but gone were the brazen girls begging to share a table with him. That was why she was able to lose herself in her reverie without interruptions.

"I've gotta do something about Lean, but I can't ignore the situation with Gil, either..."

Ultimately, she didn't know if Jade and Lean's camping trip event had succeeded or not.

Jade hadn't gotten injured protecting Lean, but they'd been tighter than ever since the trip. From an onlooker's perspective, the way they shared secrets, and the fact they got on like a house on fire, may very well have suggested they were dating.

But to Cecilia, who knew the truth, it was clear their relationship was not romantic in the slightest.

"She's not exactly avoiding events with other characters, but that doesn't mean she's trying to get close with them, either..."

While the same could be said for the other characters as well, protagonist Lean was the one who most refused to behave as expected. Since she was the main character in a dating sim, Cecilia had expected she'd act like one, but so far, it had been the opposite. She seemed to have little interest in her own love life. Instead, she was busy pairing other people off.

Cecilia ate a bite of quiche. "Anyway, I've gotta settle things with Gil first!"

He was a precious member of her family, the only person she wished to cherish more than herself. To her, Gilbert was a foster brother, a companion, and a best friend she couldn't afford to lose.

"Why is he so mad in the first place?"

She did think it was wrong of her not to mention that she'd shared a room and even a bed with Oscar, but he hadn't found out she was a girl, so what was the big deal?

That was Cecilia's take on it, so even if she *had* gotten busted, she'd expected him to give her a disgruntled lecture; she hadn't foreseen that he would be almost completely overcome with fury. She'd never seen him so angry before in her life.

"Oh, Cecil. Are you alone today?" came a voice from behind her. She turned back to find Oscar. The female students started to buzz excitedly at the sight of them together, probably partly due to the influence of Lean's book. There were even a few squeals.

You guys all have such active imaginations...

An unintentional half smile came to her lips.

Oscar knew about the novel, of course, but didn't seem bothered by it. Without asking permission, he sat down across from her at the table. Once he did, a server immediately brought a cup of coffee.

This was, after all, a dining hall for nobility. Service was much more attentive than at any café or restaurant, and the interior was impeccably decorated.

Oscar took a sip of his beverage. "You're not usually by yourself. What happened to Gilbert?"

"Just some stuff... What about you?"

"I didn't have time to eat lunch today. I'm here to distract myself," he replied, lifting his coffee.

"Distract yourself? As in from your hunger? You should get the king to help you during lunch breaks. It's not good for your health to skip so many meals," she protested.

"Yeah, but I'll have to do all this someday. Won't it be better in the future if I get used to it now? Time is a finite resource."

"I mean, I guess that's true, but still..." Cecilia sighed. She'd found out after getting to know Oscar better that he also had royal duties to carry out in addition to his studies. Naturally, those involved documents he couldn't take outside, so at lunchtime he'd return to his dorm. The king also summoned him often, so he was frequently absent for the afternoon or the whole day.

Academy courses were fairly rigorous, too, so he must have been swamped.

"You must be starving, then! Eat some of this!" she implored, stuffing a piece of bread she happened to be holding into his mouth.

"Wha—? Mmf!"

"Be sure to chew properly, or it could upset your digestion!"

"..."

Despite initial objections, he eventually started to chew the bread, then finished it off. He must have been starving.

After making sure he'd swallowed it, Cecilia broke into a grin. "Can't fight on an empty stomach, you know!"

"You just try doing that at the palace. You won't get off with just a lecture..."

"Huh? Why?"

"My food all has to be tasted."

"Ohhhh...," she realized; it was clear she'd forgotten all about that.

Every dish served at the school underwent strict inspections. Food tasters checked for poison every day, and the tableware and cutlery were managed meticulously. Considering how many children of noble families attended, it was all in the interest of preventing a worst-case scenario.

As the crown prince, Oscar even had his own personal taster. This extra precaution was taken because nothing could happen to the royal heir. The coffee he held now must have already been tested for poison before being served to him. Because no one else but him had their own taster, Cecilia had completely forgotten about it.

"Can't believe you really did the exact same thing Cecilia did..."

"Huh?"

"Nothing. Just be careful in the future," he said, the tips of his ears tinged a little red. "Anyway, why isn't Gilbert around? I thought he would've shown up by now to interrupt us."

"Interrupt...?"

"He would, wouldn't he? Normally," Oscar asserted, as if it weren't up for debate. True, whenever Cecilia spoke to Oscar, Gilbert would pop by and intrude with uncanny timing.

Cecilia just thought it all a coincidence, but Oscar seemed to believe Gilbert purposely swung by to interrupt them.

"Did you two have a fight or something?" Oscar asked, hitting the nail on the head. Cecilia gave a visible start, which he didn't fail to miss. The crown prince narrowed his eyes, scrutinizing her.

"What happened?" he asked in a gentler tone than usual, and Cecilia resigned herself to admitting the truth.

"So he's jealous."

"Jealous...?" she repeated doubtfully, stroking her chin. The thought had definitely crossed her mind—that maybe Gilbert felt like his sister was stolen from him when he read Lean's novel. But...

"But would it upset him *that* much?" she wondered. Maybe over someone he was deeply in love with, sure, but she was his sister. They were very close, but they were still siblings.

"Well, that could be just how important you are to him. I mean, wouldn't you be out of sorts if a close friend suddenly bonded with someone you hated?"

"I guess..."

She could maybe understand that. While Cecilia didn't have very many friends due to always staying home from parties to maintain her male persona, she'd had a large social circle in her previous life.

"But you two get along pretty well, right?" she asked.

"A little, I guess, although we're not best friends by any stretch. He really wants to draw a line between us," he answered. Gilbert unfailingly called Oscar "Your Highness" and used formal speech with him. Although Oscar had told him to stop, he'd refused to change his behavior.

You could see a bit of a stubborn streak there.

I didn't take him for the possessive type, though...

Gilbert acted aloof about everything as a rule. He didn't form many attachments, nor did he care much about his belongings, either. The idea of him displaying such strong devotion to her felt strange, wrong even.

But since she couldn't come up with any other explanation, she had to accept Oscar's theory.

Possessiveness, huh? I could understand if it was Gilbert from the game. There's even an event like that...

The Gilbert of the game is much gloomier in nature, doesn't open up to anyone, and refuses to go to school. Cecilia considers him the shame of the family and refuses to associate with him.

Everyone around him writes him off as a worthless shut-in, so when he is chosen as knight, they whisper behind his back that there must have been some mistake. Only Lean, the protagonist, sees something in him.

She speaks with him from the other side of the closed door to his room in the dorms, encouraging him. Occasionally, she brings him snacks and whiles away the hours with him. As she does this, he opens up to her, and she becomes the only person he lets into his heart.

But as he grows dependent on Lean, so too does his heart grow ever frailer. An Obstruction takes control of him, and his possessiveness leads him to attack the boys who are close with her.

Ultimately, Lean is also the one to stop Gilbert. Despite her injuries, she touches the mark on his skin and pleads, "I want you to go back to the sweet Gilbert I know." Released from the Obstruction, he bitterly regrets his actions and vows never to hurt her again.

Ah, that's such a moving event... Hmm? Hold on.

She realized something. "Does that mean an Obstruction will attack Gilbert if he's left alone?!"

"What are you talking about?" asked Oscar, losing the thread and staring up at Cecilia as she leaped to her feet. But she didn't have time to pay attention to him right now.

No! If I don't do something...

Panicking over her adorable little brother's predicament, she broke out into a sweat. She hoped someone would stop Obstruction-possessed Gilbert immediately, like in the game, but there was no way reality would unfold that smoothly. This past month had drilled that painful lesson into her over and over again.

Her brother had a sharp tongue, but he was a good person. If he hurt someone under the Obstruction's influence, he wouldn't be able to forgive himself for as long as he lived. What was the best course of action here?

"Lean?" she said to herself, as a face flashed in her mind like a divine revelation.

It was always Lean who rescued him. In the game, Gilbert says that he fell in love with her at first sight. Thus, his present counterpart *must* also have feelings for her deep down.

Cecilia hurriedly tidied up her dishes. Across from her, Oscar cocked his head. "Where are you going?"

"To Lean!" she answered, just as the heartless bell signaling the end of lunch rang throughout the academy.

After school, Cecilia found herself in the fine arts classroom.

Before her stood Lean, with Oscar next to her for some reason.

"So...what do you think?" asked Cecilia, with the desperate energy of someone about to fall to their knees at any moment.

"I'm not quite sure what to say..." Lean frowned, uncomfortable. "To sum everything up, your friend Lord Gilbert has been having some troubles lately, and you want me to go talk to him about that?"

"Y-yes, pretty much…"

"Why me?" Lean inquired, which was a perfectly natural thing to ask.

If he's your friend, you should be the one to counsel him.

If it were Cecilia in Lean's position, she would have thought the same.

"I mean, you just seem…like the type of person he'd open up to about anything!" Cecilia answered, clearly stringing words together as she went. It was a last-ditch excuse.

But Lean opted not to pry, merely saying, "I'm grateful if that's how you think of me… Lord Gilbert, hmm? I would very much like to help him, too, but…"

"But?"

"But actually, I'm swamped with work on my next novel," she admitted, lifting up a pile of hundreds of pages to show them. Of course, this one also featured characters based on Oscar and Cecil.

Dispirited, Cecilia could practically feel herself deflate.

"Jade says he's acquired a big print shop, and we're discussing printing books on a very large scale. So I'd like to put out something even better…"

This conversation was going off the rails fast.

Obviously, there isn't an equivalent event to this that occurs in the game. If there were, people would have complained to the game developers. What kind of dating sim has the main character printing fan-made romantic novels pairing off her own love interests with each other?

At the same time, she was the only one who could save Gilbert's soul.

"Okay, then! I'll help you!"

"What?"

"I'll help you write your story! I bet I can do stuff like collecting reference materials and proofreading! So whenever you're free, could you just talk to Gil—?"

"Oh! Oh my! My, oh my! Really?!" Lean cried, eyes sparkling as she grabbed Cecilia's hand.

"Uh, yeah..."

"In that case, as a little advance on your work, could you help me out with something now? If you agree, I'll do as you ask!"

"O-okay...," Cecilia agreed vaguely, overpowered by Lean's intensity.

Next to her, Oscar sighed. "You idiot."

"All right, you two. Bring your faces a little closer. Yes! That's it! Now place your hands on each other's shoulders! Lord Cecil, please try to give off more of a sensual feel!"

"Ah, I'm not sure I'm capable of sensual..."

"And Prince Oscar, look more like you're getting overwhelmed by him!"

"..."

Cecil and Oscar—and Lean—were behind the school. Oscar had his back to the wall, while Cecilia was posed before him to look as if she wanted to trap him.

It was like their pinned-up-against-the-wall moment from a while back, only with the roles reversed.

At Lean's direction, Cecilia had placed her leg between Oscar's knees.

"I wanted to add illustrations to the book, but without models, I simply couldn't get anything looking right! Thank you so much, Lord Cecil and Prince Oscar!"

"Mmm...," Cecilia replied dispiritedly. When she'd offered to help, she hadn't meant doing this. To the other victim, who was following Lean's commands obediently, she said, "Oscar, I'm sorry I dragged you into something weird."

"I'm fine. Unlike you, I'm just standing here." Oscar shrugged.

While they spoke, Lean held out her sketchbook, pencil frantically scratching away. She was the picture of concentration. Since they had nothing to do besides stand there, Cecilia decided to ask Oscar something she was curious about. "By the way, what did you think of that novel?"

"What novel?"

"You know, the one based on us..."

On top of it being about two boys, Cecil was a baron's son. While it would have been acceptable if the crown prince was paired with the duke's daughter, Cecilia, normally someone of that rank would've had nothing to do with a baron's son. Her guilt over whether that element offended Oscar drove her to ask him directly.

"I don't have much of an opinion on it. First of all, it's unrealistic for you to be doing this and that to me anyway. A person with noodle arms like yours couldn't force someone back using just one arm," Oscar said indifferently. It sounded like he really wasn't bothered by it at all, which relieved her.

"Right, there's no way I could push you down onto your back. Although the other way around could work."

"Yeah, the other way around would at least feel more realistic... Wait, the other way?" Oscar stuttered, momentarily freezing.

He flushed instantly. Who knew what he'd just imagined? Since her face was so close to his, Cecilia noticed it right away.

"Oscar, are you all—right?!"

The moment she tried to get a better look at his expression, he pushed her away. "Don't get so close to my face right now! You startled me! You really startled me!"

"I was just worried about you."

"I have Cecilia!"

"Not right now, though?"

"That's not what I mean!"

"I wasn't trying to say that, either," Cecilia protested.

Oscar had been acting a little strange lately. Most of the time he was his usual self, but whenever she got close to his countenance or touched him somewhere, he overreacted just like that.

It hurt a little for him to keep that distance between them even though they'd become friends and everything.

After Lean finished her sketch, she turned the page. "Next, Prince Oscar, could you undo two or three buttons? Please!"

"What? You're going to draw more?"

"Of course! I can't waste this opportunity! And Lord Cecil, insert your hand in there!"

"What?!"

"Like you're just slipping your fingertips inside his shirt! There, freeze! That's perfect. Stay just like that," she drooled, dropping her gaze back down to her sketchbook. What a shameless girl.

Frankly, posing like this with Oscar was embarrassing enough to send her to an early grave, but she thought of Gilbert and persevered.

"Okay, now I want—"

"Um, Lean?"

Cecilia turned around. On the tip of her tongue was *This is really getting too embarrassing—could we stop?*

Then she noticed who was standing beyond Lean and staring at them.

"Oh, Gil…"

It was Gilbert. Without a word, he marched right up to the three of them. Then he grabbed Cecilia's wrist.

"Hey!"

He seemed intent on silently dragging her off right there.

Oscar piped up, too. "Hey, Gilbert!"

"Your Highness, please be quiet right now. I'm in a very bad mood," Gilbert demanded, not even turning around to face him. Then he yanked Cecilia out of there.

He brought her to their usual greenhouse. Sure enough, they were the only two people there. Gilbert hadn't spoken the entire time, so Cecilia ventured meekly, "Umm…Gil?"

"What was that back there?"

"Back there, um…"

He must have meant how she and Oscar had been pressed up against each other. She flinched at his scathing tone.

"Umm, that was us helping Lean out with an illustration for her book, since she asked…"

At that, Gilbert faced his sister for the first time. His expression was even more blank and impenetrable than she'd imagined.

"Helping? She asks you to help, and you're totally fine doing *that*?"

"Well, not really…"

Of course, she wouldn't have done it if Lean had asked for it as a favor. But since Gilbert was on the line, she'd agreed. And now he was criticizing her for it.

"I'm amazed you could put yourself on display like that. Do you have no shame? Do you know what would happen if people found out that a duke's daughter was doing that without batting an eyelid?"

"Um… But I'm Cecil right now!"

"Are you sure you're not conflating 'dressed as Cecil' for 'I can do whatever I want'?" he pointed out acidly, making her cringe. That wasn't…entirely untrue.

"Even if you're dressed as Cecil, you are still a woman, and the prince is a man. Aren't you aware of a little thing called restraint?"

"But…"

"So I guess that means…," Gilbert threatened, suddenly stepping right up to her. Dropping her wrist, he wrapped a hand around her waist. This left her immobilized, unable to escape. "…I can do to you what you were doing back there?"

He brushed the thumb from his other hand over her lips.

"Wait, wha…?"

Reflexively, she tried to push against Gilbert's chest, but he wouldn't budge. As he came closer and closer, she was at a complete loss. All she could see was his face.

Hey, this is kinda… Huh? It's like he's going to kiss me… What?!

"Ngh…"

She squeezed her eyes shut, and her whole body seized up.

Then, instead of a kiss, a sigh fell on her lips.

"You get it now, right? Be more careful in the future," Gilbert chided, releasing her. Then he turned to leave.

"Gil!" she desperately called out to stop him.

"Bye," he said, leaving the greenhouse without so much as turning back.

Now I've gone and done it…

Back in his room, Gilbert was mortified and dejected. As he recalled the sensation of her lips against his thumb, his face heated up.

That was going too far for just losing my temper…

He'd decided not to do anything to make Cecilia more aware of him, and yet when he'd witnessed the two of them crossing that boundary so quickly, he'd relinquished all his self-restraint.

If Cecilia's body language hadn't made her resistance clear, he absolutely would have kissed her right then and there.

"I bet she hates me now…"

The truth of it cut deep. She had probably just closed her eyes without thinking too hard about it, but to Gilbert, her rejection was obvious.

Pressing the backs of his hands to his eyes, he let out a pathetic groan. "Aaahhhh…"

The next day, Cecilia had turned to moss.

She sat on a bench along the route from the dorms to the academy, dazed and staring at the ground.

All the students passing by noticed her abnormal state, but she appeared so unapproachable that everyone just pretended not to see.

The cause of her transformation was Gilbert, of course.

That morning, she'd gotten ready to go to school earlier than usual so she could make a proper apology to him when he came to get her as he did every morning.

He always swung by early, and since she was never ready on time, she would always end up making him wait. But today she was eager to use that time to apologize to him.

Yet today, he didn't show up—neither at his usual time nor many minutes later. Fed up, Cecilia headed for his room, but he'd already left for class.

In other words, he'd left her behind.

But this has never happened before…

They'd been brother and sister for twelve years. They'd quarreled, but they always made up the next day. This was the first fight of theirs that spanned more than a single day.

"What are you doing there?" someone asked. She looked up to find Oscar gazing down at her with a mystified look.

Her face crumpled when she saw him. "Gil…"

"Mmm?"

"Gil hates me now…," she said, bursting into tears. Oscar's eyes darted around in a panic before he evidently decided to start by sitting down next to her. Feeling the wood of the bench creak, Cecilia sniffled and turned to him.

"Just stop crying for now," he said gruffly, holding out a handkerchief.

She took it and sniffled. "What do I do? He completely hates me now."

"…Is this about yesterday?"

"That, too, but I think he's mad because he's disappointed in me over a lot of stuff."

Gilbert's statement about *"If you're dressed as Cecil..."* looped over and over in her mind.

She hadn't gone so far as to think she could do whatever she wanted dressed as Cecil. But she did feel freer as him. To hold the title of a high-ranking nobleman's daughter meant putting up with many, many more restrictions and constraints than most people lived with. No matter what she was doing, she always had to execute it with perfection.

Gilbert must have seen through to how she really felt about that.

"Well, I don't really have that many friends, so I can't say I know that much about arguments," Oscar falteringly admitted. "But if you upset him, you should apologize, right? If you know you did something wrong, give him an honest and sincere apology."

Cecilia gazed up at him. The crown prince looked even more put out than usual, probably unused to the very concept of giving someone advice.

"I contributed to what upset him, too, so I could say sorry to him, but I think it would have the opposite effect this time, right?" Oscar ventured.

"Y... Yeah."

Gilbert was mad at Cecilia, and an apology from Oscar wouldn't change that. If anything, it might make Gilbert scorn her further for making someone else apologize on her behalf.

"How do you think I should express regret to him?"

"Ah... Hmm. I'd start by bringing him something he likes, maybe?"

"Something he likes...?"

Gilbert was someone who held no real attachment to anything. He had food he preferred, sure, but he could still eat the things he didn't care for, and he wasn't particularly bothered if he couldn't scarf down his favorite meals. That attitude carried over to his material possessions and interpersonal relationships.

"What does Gil like...?" she mused.

"You can't think of anything? Like something he's treasured since childhood or his favorite food."

"Umm... Oh!" she cried, popping her head up. She'd thought of one thing—something he'd treasured for years and kept safe even now. "Oscar! Are you familiar with this?!"

"I wouldn't say I'm an expert..."

"Tell me whatever you know. I'm all ears!"

"Sigh."

Gilbert was seated on a chair in the courtyard at lunchtime. Report sheets were spread out on the table in front of him. He didn't feel like eating, so he was silently chipping away at the homework assigned during his previous period.

He couldn't stop worrying about his conversation with Cecilia from yesterday. He'd walked to school alone in the morning without coming to get her since he'd felt so awkward about it, but that ended up distressing him, too.

I probably hurt her feelings.

Even though facing her was too difficult, leaving her behind had also aggravated his feelings of guilt. To drown all that out, he focused his attention on answering his assignments.

"Lord Gilbert, is there something bothering you?" came a voice just as he was almost done. He looked up to see Lean.

"Do you need something?" he asked, uncharacteristically curt. Though Gilbert outranked her in terms of social standing, he was faultlessly polite to everyone as a general rule. Cecilia was the only person at school he treated casually.

"I was just wondering what you're doing," she replied.

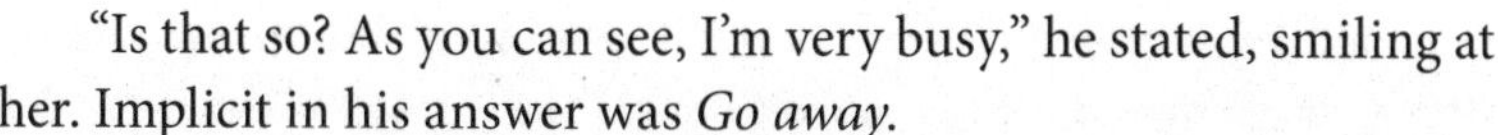

"Is that so? As you can see, I'm very busy," he stated, smiling at her. Implicit in his answer was *Go away.*

But she simply smiled back at him, undaunted. "I can wait until you're done. How about we have a little chat? I've been curious about you for so long now. I'd love to discuss all kinds of things with you..."

"Curious? Please." He snorted. There was no way Lean had any interest in him. That was obvious in her behavior this whole time.

His homework completed, Gilbert set about tidying up his pens and report sheets. "Cecil put you up to this, didn't he? To check on me or something? I'm perfectly fine, so please let me be."

"Oh. You've seen right through everything, then." Lean giggled, admitting it quite indifferently.

As he cast a sidelong glance at her, he continued putting away his school supplies. "While Cecil may be an utter fool, he wouldn't offer to assist you with something untoward of his own accord. If he did, it would be in exchange for something else. So he told you to come talk to me in return for him helping you, didn't he? Because he thinks I like you or something..."

"I'd hate for you to get the wrong idea. It was Cecil who first proposed doing something in exchange."

"I can tell as much," he grumbled, irritation building into a headache thanks to this conversation.

Cecilia was always whining about Lean not acting as she expected her to, and indeed, she would never act in compliance with the whims of others. If anything, she made other people bend to *her* whims.

"Were you upset to see them posing like that?" Lean inquired.

"That has nothing to do with you, does it?" he retorted, displeased at how she made it sound as if she'd read his emotions.

"Lord Cecil really is a fool, isn't he?" she commented.

Gilbert had let all this slide off his back so far, but that one offended him. It was one thing for *him* to point out Cecilia's flaws, but he'd be *damned* if he let anyone else do it. He threw Lean a fierce glare without saying a word.

But Lean kept that same placid smile on her face, not intimidated by him in the slightest. "Don't you think you're being presumptuous trying to get him to realize things on his own? At the moment, he doesn't have the presence of mind to notice feelings that you haven't conveyed to him."

"What are you implying?"

"I'm only saying that if you're planning on apologizing, you should do it quickly."

"......"

"And give me a more interesting story to work with," she demanded with finality, sweeping into a ladylike curtsy before turning on her heel to leave. Then she looked back over her shoulder charmingly and added, "Oh, that's right. I forgot to ask you something. Lord Cecil hasn't come to class all day today. Do you know anything about that?"

"Excuse me?"

After a pregnant pause, she added, "I do hope he's all right. The world can be such a dangerous place."

Then Lean left, having said her piece and nothing more.

Her words struck true, gnawing at Gilbert from the inside out. "She didn't go to class? That can't be right!"

At her core, Cecilia was dedicated and earnest. It was difficult to conceive of her missing school for no reason. Did something more important come up, or had something prevented her from going? From a logical standpoint, it had to be one of those two scenarios.

The possibility of the Killer flitted through his mind.

That mysterious murderer of potential Holy Maidens. If the Killer had attacked her...

Once he got on that train of thought, he could remain still no longer.

I'll just go to her room to check, Gilbert thought, getting to his feet. His face was the picture of calm, but sweat had started to bead on his forehead.

"Maybe she just stayed home because she's not feeling well today," he reasoned, attempting to reassure himself.

He shouldn't have been panicking so much, but images of the worst-case scenarios kept filling his thoughts.

In the game, Cecilia is found with a knife through her heart, or drowned in a river, or hanged in the mountains...

All those tragedies played out in his mind with the face of the sister he knew. It was so chilling that he found it hard to breathe.

After he exited the courtyard, turned down a corridor, and was almost out of the school building, he ran into the one person he didn't want to see that day.

"There you are, Gilbert."

"Your Highness...," he hissed, the words coming out in a groan despite himself. That made Oscar squint at Gilbert for just a second before he blinked and returned to a mild expression. Gilbert tried to rush past Oscar to get to the dorms.

"Hey, don't ignore me," he demanded, catching hold of Gilbert's arm to stop him from running away.

Gilbert shrugged him off. "I'm in a hurry!"

He'd never spoken or acted so roughly with Oscar before. Because he would one day serve the king as his subject, he wanted to keep their relationship nominally pleasant. His own sense of self-interest, along with a cost-benefit analysis, had informed all their interactions up until now. Currently, however, being level-headed was beyond him.

Oscar merely sighed, evidently not offended in the slightest. "I didn't know you could be so emotional."

"Oh, really? I've always been like this. Now, if you'll excuse me."

"I'm telling you to hold on a second!" he protested, blocking the path.

"Get out of my way!" Gilbert roared. Fortunately, there was no one else around to witness their spat, because gossip-hungry nobles would have delighted in witnessing the crown prince laying into the duke's son.

"Listen to me; it's about Cecil," Oscar managed, which made Gilbert freeze in place. "He's in the nurse's office right now. I just wanted to tell you—"

"He's not hurt, is he?!" Gilbert interrupted loudly. Alarm bells clanged in his head as he jumped to the conclusion that the Killer had actually attacked her.

"Yeah, but—"

As soon as Gilbert heard that, he reversed directions and took off. Oscar trailed close behind, shouting at him to stop, but this time Gilbert ignored his pleas. As the door to the nurse's office came into view, he put on a burst of speed. Without checking to see who was inside, he opened the door and shouted out, "Sister!"

Only Cecilia was inside, sitting on a stool with her back to the door. He could make out the edges of white gauze patches on her face and a bandage wrapped around her ankle.

"Oh, Gil!" she cried, turning to face him with a joyous look on her face.

Once he saw she was safe and sound, Gilbert slumped against the wall. Though he covered his face in one hand, his expression was one of sheer relief. "Thank goodness…"

"What's going on?"

"Ah, I just heard from Lean that you hadn't come to classes today. I got worried that maybe the Killer had done something to you…"

"Gil…," she trailed off, guilt flashing across her visage as she saw him express rare, genuine concern for her.

"You didn't get attacked, right?"

"Nope. My own clumsiness did this to me…"

"What do you mean? What did you do?"

She giggled sheepishly. "Fell down the side of a mountain."

"WHAT?!"

On closer inspection, he saw that her school uniform was caked in dirt and that leaves were still stuck in her wig.

"But thanks to my hike, I was able to find this. Here!" she announced proudly, lifting up a potted gentian flower that had been sitting on the floor.

Something clicked for him. "Wait, you don't mean you went and picked that?!"

"Yup. I remembered that you've never been very attached to anything, except for the gentian I gave you a long time ago. You even pressed it into a bookmark to keep forever, so I thought you must really love them!"

There in the pot bloomed a flower that was just like the one she'd given him as a kid.

"This time I dug up the roots, too! That way you can enjoy looking at it for longer, right?!"

"That's why you skipped class and got all dinged up? ...You really are stupid," he said, despite an irrepressible smile curving his lips upward. While his grin was at war with the furrow in his brow, right now, happiness was winning out.

That happiness all stemmed not from the gentian but from the fact that she'd remembered something from so long ago.

Cecilia held the flowerpot out to her brother, bowing her head low. "Gil, I'm so sorry. I guess I really thought that nothing was off-limits as long as I'm Cecil. That was shortsighted of me, so I understand why you got upset."

"I..."

"Also, I know you wanted me to pay attention to you, too, and not just Oscar! You felt left out!"

His eyes narrowed as she suddenly switched to treating him

like a kid. It really drove home that no matter what he did, he would always be her baby brother. But before he could feel too sorry for himself, what happened next completely derailed his pity party.

Cecilia threw her arms around him in a hug, then rubbed his back like she used to when they were kids. "Sorry, Gil. I'm sorry I'm such a good-for-nothing sister."

At that moment, what Lean had told him rang in his ears: *"Don't you think you're being presumptuous trying to get him to realize things on his own? At the moment, he doesn't have the presence of mind to notice feelings that you haven't conveyed to him."*

Gilbert wrapped his arms around her back and pulled her in close. She gave him a soft, sisterly smile, as he knew she would.

"Um…so I love you," he blurted out, the words sounding more stilted than he'd intended. But once he started, he found his emotions were pouring out of him like tea from a cracked cup.

"That's why I objected so much to finding you with His Highness, and got angry, and said all that. I hate seeing another man touch you."

"Gil?"

"I love you. I really do."

She stared up at him in shock for a while, frozen on the spot. Then, like ice melting, a warm smile spread across her face, and she hugged Gilbert tight. "I looove you, too! I really do. You mean the world to me!"

Her response hadn't been romantic—it was what you'd say to your brother. But for some reason, it wasn't that disheartening.

I suppose that's all right for now.

If that was how things were, Gilbert would just have to keep being proactive and pursuing her until she realized the truth. Deep inside his heart, he tore up the vows he'd made to avoid making a move or telling her how he felt. He no longer needed to hesitate. In the end, making one attempt or a hundred would amount to the same thing.

But there was one final thing he wanted to confirm. "Who do you like better, me or the prince?"

"You or Oscar?" she asked, blinking. "You, of course!"

She declared this without an iota of hesitation. He felt as though a weight had lifted right off his chest.

"Hey, Cecilia, I love you."

"Yeah. I love you, too, Gil! I love you the most!"

He knew she didn't mean it romantically. Cecilia's feelings for him were of a sister toward her brother.

But that was fine. At the very least, he was the one she loved the most for now.

Now he just had to gradually wear her down until he'd wrapped her around his little finger.

"If you're done getting treated, want to head back? I'll walk you to your classroom."

"Okay. Oh, but wait up!" she cried, rushing to start getting ready to go.

Like hell I'd let that disgusting prince take her from me, Gilbert vowed bitterly.

"Oh my! How very lovey-dovey!" Lean whispered, peeping in on Gilbert and Cecil from a crack in the door. She made a rectangle with her fingers and captured them inside it.

"I can just feel the creative juices flowing!" she said excitedly, her entire body vibrating.

She knew that Oscar had brought Cecil to the infirmary, as she'd happened to see them going in together. That was why she'd given Gilbert a little nudge. She'd been hoping to see a bit of drama, but what she ended up with honestly exceeded even her wildest expectations.

Someone approached her. "What are you doing there?"

"Oh, Prince Oscar. Did you just get here? I'm afraid you've missed out on a wonderful little scene," Lean informed him, grinning from ear to ear and clutching her sketchbook.

He took one look at it and snapped disapprovingly, "You're going to make *another* one?"

"Yes! And it may be my best work yet! I'll have to get Jade's help as well!"

"Just don't go overboard."

"Mm-hmm!" she chirped, full of energy and in high spirits.

Shortly afterward, novels and stories about Gilbert and Cecil's close bond flourished in the library...

✦ CHAPTER 5 ✦ Cecilia Gets Kidnapped

"So I was thinking… Maybe this world isn't the setting of the game that I knew?"

"If you have time to chat, you have time to work."

It was late May, and class had let out. Happily reconciled, Gilbert and Cecilia were sitting across from each other at a table in the dining hall, surrounded by textbooks and notebooks.

Yes, they were right in the middle of studying for midterms.

"Hey! Gil, I'm being serious here—listen to me!"

"And I'm saying get serious about studying. It's all over if you can't make any progress without me tutoring you, and I'm a year below you."

"I know…" She pouted. They were in the common space of the dining hall, so she was being careful not to say anything that would give away that she was a girl.

It was not because Cecilia was a bad student that she was studying so hard for midterms. Despite her tendency to catastrophize straight to doomsday scenarios, she was intelligent enough. Her grades were always among the highest in the academy.

No, the reason she was studying so frantically now was because of the academic system at Vleugel Academy. Scholastic excellence was a given here since it had been established for the purposes of educating fine ladies and gentlemen of noble stock. Accordingly, if any student dropped more than five places between exams in the class ranking, their parents would be contacted. Depending on the circumstances, a home visit from the teacher could even be warranted.

Only the academy higher-ups knew that Cecilia was attending dressed as a boy, and all her teachers only knew her as Cecil. That meant that if a home visit occurred, her parents would find out about her cross-dressing exploits.

No matter how doting her parents were, they still wouldn't allow their daughter to attend class while dressed as a man.

Incidentally, even though Gilbert never acted like he was studying particularly hard, his ranking only ever fluctuated between first and third place in his year.

"So… What were you going to say?" he asked.

"You'll listen to me?"

"If I don't, you'll just be annoying about it later." He sighed.

Her brother really was sweet. After checking to make sure no one was nearby, she lowered her voice. "I think there's just too many differences from the game world that I know. I can understand why your personality is different, but Oscar and Jade are a bit off, too, and the Killer hasn't shown up… Plus, Lean is the most different of all. The version I know never behaves this aggressively."

Lean Rhazaloa was someone who always wore an angelic smile. She was a girl so sweet and ephemeral that everyone in the game felt an instinctual need to protect her.

But the Lean of this world appeared to be running completely wild. She was crafty, drew everyone into her schemes, and did exactly what she wanted.

"But she still has to get together with someone, right? At this point, who's a possibility?"

"Umm, let's see…"

Cecilia carefully wrote down the names of the love interests in her notebook: Oscar; Gilbert; Jade; Mordred, the school doctor; Oscar's friend Dante; and the twins, Eins and Zwei.

"Out of these, Oscar kinda seems the most likely. Plus, he seems to be into her..."

"Mmm. He's out."

"Huh?"

"Not that I want to help my enemy out or anything, but I don't want you going on a fool's errand. There's no way it'll be His Highness," he declared flatly.

Cecilia's eyes widened with shock. "Why not?!"

"Because I said so. Although I'm personally hoping he'll get distracted, too."

"Talking about me?" interjected none other than Oscar, who had approached them. Next to him stood an unfamiliar face...

"Dante?!"

Dante Hampton, one of the love interests. His hair was a bright and eccentric blend of green and blue, and he wore an insincere smile, a choker at his neck, and a half-undone school uniform. He seemed the opposite of an ideal student in every respect.

"What are you doing?" asked Oscar.

"What does it look like? We're studying. Midterms are coming up, and we're preparing," Gilbert snapped back. Previously, he would have kept a smile pasted on his face despite the effort, but now he wore the same surly look that he might show to Cecilia. For anyone else, it would be the other way around, but this was a sure sign that Gilbert had warmed up to Oscar.

But it was Dante who reacted. "Hey, Oscar, let's join them."

"Hmm?"

"*What?*" spat Gilbert with obvious revulsion, glaring at Dante.

But the subject of his ire was undeterred. "We were just talking about studying, weren't we?"

"Yeah, I guess we were," answered Oscar.

"So how about it, O famous prince of the school?" Dante drawled, with that last bit directed at Cecilia.

"Umm... Sure. Okay, we can study together," she agreed, feeling it would be strange to refuse. In all honesty, however, she didn't want to interact with any more love interests if she could help it.

"Great!" shouted Dante, immediately dragging the neighboring table right up to theirs before sitting next to Cecilia. Left with no alternative, Oscar sat down next to Gilbert.

"Now that I'm sizing you up from close quarters, I can see you really are as pretty as all the rumors say," marveled Dante, staring at Cecilia as he set his books and notepads on the table.

Under his peculiar gaze, she gave a noncommittal nod. "Mmm."

"*And* you've got the future king and prime minister eating out of the palm of your hand!" Dante gasped.

Both Gilbert and Oscar broke into coughing fits at that. Their eyes both turned red-rimmed.

Dante scooted closer to Cecilia. "But y'know..."

He gave her a once-over, appraising her like a piece of meat. She flinched uncomfortably.

"What's a pretty girl like you doing going to school dressed like a guy?"

Cecilia's body turned to ice.

"*Girl?*" said Oscar, reacting the fastest. He turned to look at her.

Cecilia grew flustered as he scrutinized her. "Umm..."

"What are you—?"

"What are you talking about? Yeah, he's got a girlie face, but he's a guy through and through," Oscar retorted before Gilbert could jump in to help.

Dante's eyes widened, like he hadn't been expecting that. "What? But no matter how you slice it..."

"I mean, yeah, he has a girl's face. But he's pretty self-conscious about it, so don't harp on it."

Dante's gaze flicked between Oscar and Cecilia. After glancing over at a stony-looking Gilbert, too, he said, "Hmm. I see."

His nod sent a shiver of fear down her spine. But Dante dropped the subject and opened his notebook. "Well, if you say so, Oscar, I guess that's how it is! Sorry, Cecil. Looks like I got it all mixed up. Did that rub you the wrong way?"

"No… I'm fine," Cecilia replied, her face pallid.

She and her brother wore equally wooden expressions for the rest of their study session.

"He knows! Dante is definitely on to me!"

"I mean, considering that reaction…"

That night, the two of them held an emergency strategy meeting in the dorm lounge. Normally, they would hold those meetings in Cecilia's or Gilbert's room, out of the public eye. But Gilbert had refused, so they'd opted for the sparsely populated lounge.

According to Gilbert, *"I don't want to be alone with you in a room with a bed if at all possible."*

He'd also told her that he was at an age where it would be hard for him to keep himself in check, but Cecilia didn't understand what he meant at all. She decided it must have been some sort of puberty thing.

No one else was in the lounge. In the period before midterms, there weren't many students complacent enough to just hang out and chat in common spaces.

Cecilia nodded, despondent. "We need to do something to keep him quiet…"

"That's a dangerous line of thought."

"Why do problems keep popping up one after another when I still need to do something about Lean's love life?!"

"Not to mention that exams are coming up."

"Aaaaaargh!" Cecilia cried, reaching her wit's end after his interjection. She always seemed to have a million problems on her plate.

"Oh, right. Dante is a knight, so he's a love interest, too, isn't he? What about Lean and Dante together? Sounds good, right?"

"Mmm, Dante?" Cecilia considered, unusually reluctant.

"Is there some problem? Does he not get a route with her?"

"No, that's not it. Actually, they get along well, but…"

"But?"

"Dante is…kind of on hard mode."

While he claims to be the third son of the Hampton family, that turns out to be merely a cover. In reality, he's an assassin from a bordering nation sent to kill Oscar.

But by the time the game opens, Dante chooses to stick with Oscar purely as his friend, the end result of electing to maintain their relationship over his duty as an assassin. Accordingly, his route primarily revolves around his struggle to decide between friendship with Oscar or the mission for his country.

During a certain event, Lean finds out he's been sent to eliminate Oscar, which also puts a target on her back. But he can't bring himself to kill her. He has innumerable opportunities to do so, but he's never able to go through with it. This causes him to mull over what's stopping him from doing her in. At long last, he arrives at a single conclusion—he's in love with her.

From that point on, he decides to wash his hands completely of the assassin life, but…

"Anyway, so that's how his route goes…"

"Okay. I need to give you a lecture." Gilbert sighed, five seconds away from blowing his lid completely.

"Why?!" she yelped.

"You should know why! Why did you just ignore such an obviously dangerous character?! I can see why you didn't tell anyone else, but at least tell me!"

"But, I mean, none of that ever comes up unless you play

Dante's route. What if I told you, and then he gets arrested? Wouldn't you feel sorry for him?"

"No, I would not!" he snapped, and Cecilia ducked her head. "Well, anyway...there's a lot to consider, but I get it. For now, I see where you're coming from. So what did you mean when you said it's on hard mode?"

"Um, so the choices in Dante's route are really harsh. Typically, a love interest's affection for you just goes down if you pick the wrong dialogue option, but in Dante's route, you die."

"What?"

"I mean, Lean dies. Because he kills her."

"..."

"And once Lean dies, it's usually Cecilia who gets blamed for it, and then she dies, too. Either in jail or from getting executed..."

Gilbert buried his face in his hands. His long sigh was just scary. "Why is this game so focused on life and death?"

"There's a lot of dating sims like that lately," she informed him.

"I wouldn't know. Nor do I care."

He lifted his head, a look of exhaustion on his face. Despite that, it seemed like he'd processed the situation.

Cecilia rubbed the furrow between her brows that had developed at some point. "So that's why I want to keep Lean from going down Dante's route if possible. If she messes a choice up, I'll go down along with her..."

"That's true. Let's avoid Dante's route at all costs, then," he agreed, nodding deeply.

"The dialogue choices influence whether Lean learns Dante's secret or not..."

"What makes that choice pop up?"

"If his affection points reach a certain threshold, Dante's junior Huey transfers in. Then Lean happens to see Huey hounding Dante about getting back to his hit-man gig."

Huey doesn't notice Lean hiding in the shadows, but Dante does. From then on, he starts threatening her.

"So what you're saying is that if this Huey guy transfers in, that's a sign of danger?"

"Yeah, that's basically it."

As usual, Gilbert's powers of comprehension were stunning. He massaged his temples, wearing a grave expression. "And we also need to come up with some sort of plan to address how he knows you're a girl. My head hurts a little."

"Sorry?"

"It's nothing you need to apologize for."

"Okay... But Lean probably has no interest in Dante. She hasn't shown any signs of it so far!" Cecilia added reassuringly.

However...

"I'm Huey Cranebel. It's nice to meet you."

The next day, Huey transferred into Cecilia's class.

It was clear and sunny that day, the exact opposite of Cecilia's mood.

"What am I gonna do...?" she moaned, gazing up at the sky through the greenhouse windows.

Gilbert was right there next to her, as usual. "I thought Lean wasn't supposed to be interested in Dante."

"Yeah, she wasn't supposed to be..."

Cecilia had meant to keep a close eye on Lean. But here in the real world, she couldn't exactly see the affection points and dialogue from the game. Furthermore, Cecilia honestly hadn't been able to check up on Lean like before, what with her fight with Gilbert and studying for exams. Lean must have gotten close to Dante in the interim.

Gilbert thumbed his lips pensively. "This Huey guy… Is he pretty much harmless?"

"Yeah. He's like a sort of apprentice assassin, so there shouldn't be any dangerous events involving him…"

Huey Cranebel, age sixteen, Dante's junior in their organization. He's supposed to be the same academic year as Gilbert, but he fudges his age in order to speak with Dante and transfer into a second-year class.

Even though he's a side character, he has an adorable appearance, and a famous voice actor provides his lines. This ensured his popularity persisted, despite not getting a route in the fan disc.

Oh, that's right, Ichika also loved Huey…

Cecilia reminisced about her past life. Even though Ichika made BL ships out of everyone and everything, Huey alone occupied a special place in her heart.

"Huey is sooooo cute! So, so cute! Hiyono, have I always been into the cute younger guy type?! Oh my god, whenever he looks at me, I just lose it!"

"Wow, this is new for you. But, Ichika, you don't usually ship yourself with the guys, do you?"

"No! I didn't think I did anyway! I guess he's just so cute he's got me all messed up!"

The way she pressed a hand to her heart and freaked out over the character was truly adorable. She went on to play through Dante's route and would replay scenes and events with Huey over and over.

Awww, good times. If Ichika were here now, she'd be so thrilled. She'd squeal, "Real Huey!"

"So what should we do? Lean's going to end up on Dante's route if we don't stop this, right?" Gilbert asked, pulling Cecilia back to reality. Right, she didn't have time to wallow in her emotions.

"But what would be the best thing to even do?"

"Keep watching from the sidelines?" he suggested.

"That seems too risky…"

Frankly, it's impossible to make it through Dante's route without consulting online guides. Hiyono messed up on his route time and time again, too, while wishing she had more fingers to juggle all the tabbing between walk-throughs. It was downright odd in the first place how there could be such a difference between choosing "Do your best" and "Do your best, okay?"

If you pick "Do your best," you survive, but selecting "Do your best, okay?" seals your doom. It was brutal.

Yet, no matter how Cecilia racked her brain, she couldn't come up with a good plan for averting Dante's route.

After deliberating for a while, Gilbert finally looked up. "Hey. Even though Huey's showed up, the route won't start unless Lean's figured out who Dante really is, right?"

"Yeah..."

"So we just have to prevent that, don't we?"

"Prevent it?" Cecilia parroted, unsure of what he meant.

"We only need to prevent Lean from overhearing Dante and Huey's disagreement. If we do that, she won't learn his identity, so he'll have no reason to target her."

"Oh! Yeah, that could work!" she cried, clapping her hands at her brother's ingenious plan.

After school, the two of them met up in the courtyard to follow Gilbert's scheme, since they knew the event happened at that time and place on the day Huey transferred in.

But the Vleugel Academy courtyard was huge, so they divided up. One would watch the south side, and the other would take the north side. When Lean showed up, whoever saw her would chase her away.

In the southern edge of the courtyard, Cecilia hid in the shade of a bower.

I've gotta make sure to drive her out!

But no matter how long she waited, Lean didn't show.

Is the event happening over where Gilbert is?

Cecilia strained her eyes, but the courtyard was too spacious, and the trees cut off her line of sight. She couldn't see all the way over to him, but she also couldn't leave her post, so her only recourse was to stay there and wait.

Lean's plenty late now. I'm going to go over to Gil's side.

Tired of waiting, Cecilia moved to stand up, but that was when Huey and Dante entered through the southern courtyard entrance. She hurried to crouch back down.

What?! But Lean isn't here yet!

In the game, Huey and Dante appear when Lean is reading under the shade of a tree after school. Cecilia looked all around but couldn't find her anywhere. Meanwhile, the two boys had started to argue.

Oh crap, am I screwed?

If Lean waltzed through the entrance right now, they'd definitely spot her—the exact situation Cecilia needed to prevent.

Wait, aren't I right where Lean was?

The woman hiding in the trees was different, but the circumstances were otherwise 100 percent identical.

As their verbal sparring continued, Cecilia hunched down even lower.

"Whatever, I don't care anymore!"

Once the discussion fell through, Huey spun on his heel and stomped out of the area. She'd at least escaped the danger of both of them encountering Lean simultaneously. As some of the tension drained from her shoulders, a few beads of sweat rolled down her back.

I think what happened next in the game is Dante finding Lean hiding in the bushes...

He'd peered into the shadows under the trees and smiled enigmatically.

"What do you think you're doing there?"

"Yes, that's the line, 'What do you think you're doing there?'— AAHHH!"

She scrambled to put distance between herself and Dante, who was peering down at her. He wore the same enigmatic smile from the game event plastered across his face.

"D-D-D-D-Dante?!"

"You're very naughty, eavesdropping like this."

Even the line is exactly the same!

He said what he should have directed at Lean, then traced his lower lip. "Don't tell me… You saw everything?"

"What? N-no, nothing! I saw nothing! I heard nothing!" she squeaked in denial, her face lined with panic. But her body language clearly indicated otherwise.

"Hmmm."

In the game, his affection for Lean is high so he doesn't kill her, but now…

She was Cecilia. Forget affection—she'd never even spoken to him before yesterday.

Think. I have to do something…

She couldn't get herself done in now. Dante hadn't quit being an assassin yet. He had no misgivings about the general concept of murder; it was only Oscar who he wanted to avoid killing at the moment.

In other words, the second Dante deemed Cecil a liability, he wouldn't hesitate to strike him down.

Cecilia decided to make an all-or-nothing gamble. In a shaky voice, she announced, "Dante, I know everything."

"Everything?"

"Yeah, including what you just discussed and more. I know the crown prince of Janis ordered you to come here, I know your assassin organization is named Heimat…"

The more details she added to that impressive list, the blanker Dante's face got, until his lack of expression was so frightening that she shivered. But faltering here would only have the opposite effect.

"I know even more damning facts about you, too."

"Hmmm."

"But I don't intend on telling them to anyone."

His eyes narrowed, watching for her move.

"So I propose a deal."

"A deal? You want money or something? I don't need a deal. I can just kill you right here," he barked in an uncharacteristically low, rough voice.

She gulped, swallowing the saliva pooling in her mouth. "Do you think I haven't taken any contingencies toward you with the knowledge I have?"

"Contingencies?"

"Another person has stored all the info I have on you. If I die, it all goes public. So you should watch how you treat me."

Dante scowled, then tapped a finger against his forehead thoughtfully. "Doesn't…seem like you're bluffing."

That's because she wasn't. She'd exaggerated a little, but if she died, then Gilbert would make everything she'd told him public.

He sighed, defeated. "What sort of deal? What do you want me to do for you?"

"Uh…"

I actually just want him to let me go free… But…

That wouldn't work. He wouldn't buy that being all she wanted.

She looked up at him, determined. "You figured out I'm a girl, didn't you?"

"Yeah," he answered without even hesitating. He really had busted her.

In a dignified voice, she continued, "I'm here as a boy on the basis of certain info in my possession. So keep your mouth shut about me being a girl. In exchange, I'll keep your secret."

"That's it?" he asked, as though he'd been let down.

"That's it, but... You want me to make you do even more?"

"Nope," he responded with a shrug, going back to his usual flippancy. "I like you, Cecil. We're mutual accomplices from now on. Don't disappoint me."

"Y-yeah."

Did I pick the wrong dialogue option...? Cecilia wondered, unable to do anything but shake Dante's proffered hand.

Several days later...

"Here, Huey. Say ahhh."

"Hey! Lean, stop it! There are people around!"

"What? So you're not going to eat it? But I worked so hard to make it..."

"Don't make such a sad face at me... Fine, I'll eat it."

"Really?! Okay, say ahhh!"

"What's going on over there?"

"Dunno."

Lean and the new transfer Huey were putting on quite a romantic show in the dining hall. Wrapped in this aura of mutual love, they snacked from a lunch Lean had prepared.

Gilbert and Cecilia gloomily watched on from a small two-person table.

"So since Lean never ended up making an entrance, that means she didn't start Dante's route?"

"Yup. I'm really glad it didn't reach the kidnapping part."

"Kidnapping?" Gilbert gasped, thrown off by yet another alarming word popping up out of nowhere.

"If Lean keeps going down Dante's route, Heimat members will kidnap her as revenge for her part in getting him to leave the organization."

Aware of his feelings for Lean, Dante attempts to call the assassination life quits. But there's no way his employers would let that slide, so they abduct Lean for ransom money and as recompense for Dante's actions.

When that happens, Dante will rescue her if his affection points are high enough; mess up even slightly on the dialogue choices before that point, however, and either Lean alone or both of them will wind up dead.

In that section of the game, even experienced dating sim players can get locked into a bad ending. But in this world, affection points and dialogue choices weren't visible, hiking up the difficulty even further.

"The game developers really don't want you to finish Dante's route all in one go. Meanwhile, *we* only get one shot at life!"

"I guess, but I'm just glad that's been avoided. We have to do something about the situation with Dante knowing you're a girl, so we can't waste all our energy on this."

"Oh, we might not need to anymore."

"What? Why?"

"Well...," she said, starting to explain before realizing that Gilbert would get mad if she told him about the deal. Ever the loyal little brother, he absolutely loathed when his big sister did anything even remotely dangerous.

"Seriously, why? Don't tell me you..." Gilbert trailed off suspiciously, sensing something from his sister's behavior.

But before he could finish, someone called out cheerfully, "Cecil!"

Something bumped against the back of her chair, causing her to lean away from it involuntarily. Looking back over her shoulder, she found Dante, smiling, with Oscar behind him.

"Having lunch now? Mind if we join you?"

"Uh, go ahead..."

"Great!" he chirped, jamming another table up against theirs, just as he had the other day, and seating himself next to her. The whole process took only five seconds. He worked so fast that neither Gilbert nor Oscar could get a word in edgewise.

"I see you went with the pasta, Cecil. I almost got that one, too."

"Um…yeah," she responded, eyeing him suspiciously as he got unnaturally close to her.

"Dante, what do you think you're doing?" she hissed, conscious of Oscar and Gilbert's questioning stares.

"What? I told you—I like you. I've never met a girl who'd strike a deal with me like you did. I definitely wanna get to know you."

"You're teasing me."

"No, I'm having fun."

"That's the same thing." She sighed.

But despite all that, their terms seemed to be in effect. Dante didn't seem like he was going to harm her in any way.

"So actually, I thought of an interesting game this morning."

"An interesting game? Hey—eeyaahh!"

He'd suddenly stroked his fingers over her knee, making her jerk. She glared at him as he smirked back at Oscar and Gilbert in amusement. Both of them had stiffened when they'd heard Cecilia's yelp.

Dante stifled a laugh. "Oh man, that's too funny. What's with that…?"

"What's with what?"

"You don't need to know, Cecil," he purred, tracing a line from her shoulder and up her neck this time.

"Argh! Dante! That tickles!"

"Sorry, sorry," he responded, not sounding remorseful in the least. As soon as he said that, he darted his hand out toward her side.

"Hey! Don't tickle my sides! I'm ticklish there—"

The sound of metal scraping across a plate rang out. Gilbert and Oscar had both stabbed their forks into their meat at the same time.

Oscar got up and grabbed Dante by the collar. "Dante, it doesn't look like you can concentrate on your meal there. Let's change places."

"Huh?"

"We're changing places," Oscar insisted again, the top half of his face shadowed.

Dante blinked and then burst out laughing. "Awww, if the prince says so, I guess I have to. You should've just said you wanted to sit next to Cecil!"

"No! I—"

"Uh-huh, yeah. Go on—go right ahead." Dante acquiesced with a wave of his hand, settling in next to Gilbert.

Oscar sat down next to Cecilia. Dante was now laughing while holding his sides. Both of the other boys' reactions must have delighted him.

Cecilia was relieved to no longer have him on top of her. She tugged on Oscar's sleeve. "Thanks, Oscar. You saved me, right?"

"I—I guess. I'm the one who brought him here and all."

"You really did save me. All Dante ever does is harass me," she whispered, embarrassed.

Oscar's cheeks turned a faint pink.

Gilbert tore his bread to pieces as he watched their little scene.

"Oh, are you jealous?" jeered Dante, observing her brother keenly. Now he had the nerve to derive entertainment from Gilbert's reaction.

"Tch," Gilbert spat dismissively.

Dante shuddered. "Cecil! Your friend is super-scary! Can you believe he just clicked his tongue at me?"

Annoyed and irritated, Gilbert ignored Dante and focused on his meal.

"He's not scary. He's a really good kid—there's no way he could be intimidating," Cecilia said.

"You two are seriously so close," piped up Oscar.

Cecilia nodded. "Yup, we are. I love Gil a lot!"

"Cecil...," Gilbert whispered, incredibly moved.

Dante poked Gilbert in the side. "Why do you look so happy?"

"Shut up, you shameless piece of shit."

"Cecil! Now he just called me a 'shameless piece of shit'!"

"What? Gil would never use such foul language."

"That's right. He's a stickler for manners, regardless of who he's dealing with. No way he'd say that to an upperclassman," added Oscar.

"Et tu, Oscar?!" Dante yelped.

Despite everything, it was a fun lunch. Cecilia enjoyed her usual nosh with Gilbert, of course, but since she avoided society functions and didn't have many friends, it was the first time since her past life that she'd shared a lively meal with so many people she was close with.

After her shower that night, Cecilia gazed out the window of her dorm room. Stars twinkled in the sky, and a warm breeze caressed her cheeks. Once exams were over, her summer vacation fun could begin.

"Ah, today was a blast." She sighed.

The four of them had also studied for exams after lunch. With her nerves from days prior soothed, she'd gotten in some quality studying this time.

"I don't really know what'll happen with Dante, but I managed to do something about him! And I'll manage somehow with my exams, too! Yay, everything's going smoothly... Hmm?"

Suddenly, Cecilia had a realization that dispelled all her fantasies and daydreams, making her bury her head in her hands. "Ugghhh! I need to make Lean start dating someone! I can't afford to rest on my laurels! Like, yeah, the exams are important, but...ugh!"

While it was good that Lean hadn't been kidnapped, that meant she really wasn't on Dante's route. Instead of nurturing her romance, Cecilia had only gotten in the way.

"Well, that's if things proceed like they do in the game. But I hope this is the one thing that plays out as it's supposed to; otherwise, Lean and I will be in danger… Wait, huh?"

She heard a sound and peered down from her window, only to see some black shadows creeping toward the girls' dorm from the opposite end of campus.

"No, don't tell me that's…"

Dread rising in her throat, she grabbed the wig she'd left on her bed and flew out of the room.

Obscuring herself in the shadows, Cecilia sneaked into the girls' dorm in her pajamas and wig. Getting caught here while in her male disguise could have dire consequences, but you can't make an omelet without breaking a few eggs. If her hunch was right, something bad was about to go down.

She held her breath so the three figures in black wouldn't detect her. They were all cloaked in the same ebony garb from head to toe, including black cloths they'd placed over their faces to conceal their identities.

They crept soundlessly into a room on the first floor. Cecilia followed and peeked inside. The next thing she knew—

"Stop it—mmf!"

Someone surrounded by the group of shadows shouted out, only for their screams to be dampened as the group gagged them with something.

When the figures parted a little to reveal who'd tried to scream, she clapped a hand over her mouth.

Is that…Lean?!

A group of men was in the process of abducting her, covering her mouth and attempting to stuff her into a burlap sack. It looked exactly like the scene from Dante's route.

But why?! I should have interrupted his route!

Lean finds out Dante's secret, which leads to him deciding to quit Heimat, which causes the organization to kidnap her in retribution.

But Lean hadn't witnessed that one crucial event. The person who had seen it…

It was me!

She didn't know how things had gotten to this point, but if Lean's role had transferred to Cecilia, then this kidnapping was entirely in the realm of possibility. In other words, Dante had decided to quit the organization because of what Cecilia had told him, which somehow made it Lean's fault.

While these thoughts raced through her mind, they continued to cram Lean into the bag. Cecilia threw a panicked look around the vicinity. Even if she called for help, the dorms had such sophisticated soundproofing that no one would notice a small scuffle. And if she kicked up too much of a fuss, she would run the risk of the assailants panicking and hurting Lean.

This was an event in Dante's route. Anything could happen.

Oh no, what can I do? Okay, first find Gil!

Gilbert had warned her over and over, until he was blue in the face, *not* to rush headlong into peril alone. If she tried to act here all by herself, she'd have a good scolding in store for her.

But…

But they'd never make it in time if she played it safe.

"Aaahhh!" Lean shrieked. She fell down, fighting back desperately.

I can't just sit by and watch!

"Stop right there!" Cecilia cried out, marching into the room. Both the sable-cloaked men and Lean stared at her.

Besides, if they abduct Lean, I'll inevitably wind up as the villain who gets killed anyway.

That was the one outcome she had to prevent.

"Who the hell are you?!" they shouted as she approached. Cecilia fixed them with a steely gaze.

They have two objectives. Reprisal for Dante and—

She bit down hard on her lower lip so her voice wouldn't waver.

—demanding a ransom!

She tore off her wig. Her long, flowing blond hair caught on the moonlight streaming in from the window and glittered in the glow.

Cecilia mustered a calm and collected smile on her face. At this juncture, she couldn't afford to so much as flinch in their presence. She would lay out some options for them. And then all they had to do was pick one.

"I am Cecilia Sylvie, daughter of Duke Sylvie. That is my beloved friend. I demand you release her," she announced in a commanding tone. The men whispered to one another, and Lean gawked at her.

While they all stood dumbstruck, Cecilia pressed down on Lean's shoulder as she crawled out of the bag. Signaling to her with her eyes to escape, the other girl nodded and took off.

"Ah!" the men cried and tried to chase after her, but Cecilia blocked their way. These must have been the apprentices from Heimat, Dante's organization. And as one might expect of apprentices, they'd bungled the job by letting Lean get away. Assassins of Dante's caliber would have captured both of them together.

Cecilia placed her hand over her heart. "You guys are just after a ransom, aren't you? You'll be able to squeeze more money out of the parents of a duke's daughter than a baron's. My parents dote on me, after all."

No one dashed off in pursuit of Lean.

Despite her trembling, Cecilia stretched up to her full height and grinned at them daringly. "Now, you decide. Who will you take—me or her? Your boss should be happy with either of us."

The next thing she knew, one of the men had punched her in the stomach. Negotiations complete, then.

As her consciousness faded, Cecilia prayed for Lean's safety.

✦ CHAPTER 6 ✦ Cecilia Is Rescued By...?

When she came to, she was in a horse-drawn carriage. She could tell from the clip-clopping of hooves and the jolting of her transportation. The inside of the carriage was dark, as was the view outside. Its wooden door was shut tight, preventing escape. Her wrists and feet had been bound, and she was gagged so that she couldn't cry out.

From her prone position, she managed to struggle upright. Her body felt a little numb from the punch she'd taken to the gut, but it gradually faded.

They took the Sacred Artifact, too.

She wasn't sure if they knew what it was when they'd stolen it, but the bracelet she always wore was missing. Her wig was gone, too.

Is someone going to come rescue me? she thought, but she didn't have much hope of that. If Lean had gone to alert people after her escape, most of them wouldn't have realized her abductors were from Dante's organization. He and Gilbert probably would, but Gilbert had to act very carefully as a duke's son, and Dante more than likely didn't feel close enough to Cecil to bother with her of his own accord.

I'm a little bit jealous of Lean right now.

She was the heroine, designed to be the object of everyone's affections.

In contrast, Cecilia was designed to be reviled and eliminated.

The future had shifted a little due to her actions, but the basic outline most likely hadn't changed at all. She didn't doubt for a minute that if she and Lean had both been abducted, Oscar and Gilbert alike would work harder to save Lean.

Well, no point in moping about it. I've gotta find a way to escape!

If she couldn't rely on anyone else, she had no choice but to be her own rescuer. She'd known that for twelve years now. Everything she'd done had been to prepare for this moment.

Just as she gave a deep, determined nod to herself, the carriage ground to a halt. The wooden door creaked open, and a man peered inside.

"Boss, this is her."

They pushed Cecilia before the organization leader. She looked up to find a woman with bright red-and-pink hair and a distinctive scar tightening the skin of her cheek.

Their hideout appeared to be an old stone castle, and this lady sat atop its throne. Her name was Marlin Sweeney—the leader of Heimat and Dante's foster mother.

Legs haughtily crossed, she regarded Cecilia. "Hmmm."

Her gaze made it clear she was appraising a price, and her voice was an alcoholic's rasp when she asked, "And this is really Cecilia Sylvie?"

"We're looking into it now, but her features should match all descriptions," answered a man behind Cecilia. He looked much stronger than the woman on the throne in terms of physical strength, but she still kept all these men in line. Not one to be underestimated.

"I'd only wanted to get revenge on Dante, and yet here an even bigger fish jumps right into the net all on her own? Because of *friendship*? Isn't that touching," sneered Marlin, stepping down before Cecilia and tilting her head up to get a good, long look at her. "Pretty face. I bet you could bring in some good coin from the menfolk."

The scar on her face stretched taut as she smiled, which sent a shiver down Cecilia's spine. It was shocking that Marlin could suggest that when they were both women.

"But if you really are the duke's daughter, that'll never work in this country… Don't worry. I'll give you back safe and sound as long as your parents pony up the cash. That's just business sense," she reassured, her features unnervingly kind. She released Cecilia's chin.

"Lock her up until we can verify some things. She's a very important hostage. Treat her with care," Marlin ordered, jerking her chin.

"Yes, boss," grunted the man behind Cecilia, giving her back another shove. Its force was so powerful that she pitched forward onto the ground. All the men around her, who'd been eating dinner and holding cups of booze, burst out laughing. Apparently, they enjoyed the pain of others.

Yeah, go on and chuckle!

She'd only pretended to fall forward in order to get close to something shiny she spotted lying on the ground. It was a dinner knife. She lifted her heel and managed to conceal it between her shoe and her foot. It might come in handy somewhere.

"Hey, what are you doing?! Get up!" the man shouted, impatiently yanking her to her feet and escorting her to the dungeon.

The dungeon was underground. Two guards were stationed in front of the door leading down to it, though no one was posted in front of the cell they threw her into. They must have thought she'd be secure enough tied up and locked away, or they assumed that a frail duke's daughter would be too weak to resist. She didn't know which.

For now, Cecilia soothed herself with the knowledge that they were underestimating her.

The men would likely come back in several hours to bring her food. So she probably had a fair amount of time to spare, but if she was going to do something, the faster the better. Although Heimat's leader was a woman, the organization otherwise appeared to consist exclusively of men. Plus, there was the fact that Marlin had said she could *"bring in some good coin from the menfolk."* If Cecilia stayed trapped here, who knew what indignities she might suffer?

In these situations, the best course of action is to take advantage of the enemy's negligence to escape, she thought, recalling what Hans, the soldier who'd taught her everything about fighting, always told her.

Pulling the knife out from under her heel, she quickly cut through the cords on her wrists. She removed the gag as well. Now that she was free, she inspected her surroundings.

The jail cell contained a wooden desk and chair. Neither looked like they'd been repaired in a long time and were too unsteady to be of any use. She removed a leg from the chair and detached a nail sticking out of it. Then, using the chair leg as a wooden mallet, she began drilling holes into the blade of the knife.

She was absorbed in that task for close to two hours.

"Done!" she whispered. Her knife had been converted into a simple saw.

Cecilia stuck the knife in a gap in the cell door and sawed at it. Wood shavings rained down. Though the bars on the door were metal, the hinges were made of wood. They'd probably been metal originally but had rusted and been swapped out for wooden replacements to cut costs.

The saw worked well, so the latch split in two after only a few minutes.

"Yay! Next, I need clothes for a disguise."

She tapped the knife against the prison bars. Alerted by the sudden clanging, a man stationed at the top of the stairs stomped down to investigate. Finding Cecilia sprawled out on the floor of her cell, he called out, "Hey! You all right?"

He was panicked, likely afraid that their precious hostage had fainted. The moment before he opened the door, he noticed that the latch had split apart. "What the—?"

"Hah!"

While he was distracted by the broken latch, Cecilia seized the opportunity and slammed him against the door. The iron portal swung open with enough force to pummel the man's forehead. As he stumbled, Cecilia kicked him right in the jewels.

"Guh!"

He squatted down as he clutched his crotch, unable to speak. For the finishing blow, Cecilia brought the wooden chair that now had three legs down on the back of his head.

"Not too bad for my first time," she said, heaving a long sigh and eyeing the guard lying prone on the ground. Quick as a flash, she stripped him of his clothes, then exchanged her pajamas for his uniform.

The idea of an assassins' organization had filled her with trepidation, but this fallen ruffian was no master hit man like Dante. He was more like a wannabe tough guy bandit.

Oh, right—doesn't the game treat Dante like an elite member?

A child born to kill—that's how he describes himself. In the game, his combat prowess is a cut above the rest. That knowledge felt worlds apart from the boy she knew now.

Clad in the miscreant's uniform, Cecilia ascended the stairs. In an area along the way, she found her missing Sacred Artifact, plus a wig that had been carelessly tossed aside.

"Yay!"

With practiced movements, she tucked her long hair up under the wig. With that, she'd transformed into a dashing young man. She still had a bit of a high-class aura, but regardless, her getup should prevent her from getting immediately recognized as an outsider.

Next, she donned the Sacred Artifact, touching it lightly before feeling a cushy barrier envelop her.

"There, that's a relief."

She was grateful to no longer need to worry about sustaining injuries. But the Artifact's power didn't make her invincible. Its effect would wear off in thirty minutes if she didn't touch it in that time, and it would also shut down if she lost consciousness. She had to keep touching it regularly.

Cecilia picked up a sweeper brush for cleaning on the ground nearby and spun it. The tool would make for a perfect impromptu weapon.

She continued up the staircase. When she reached the door, she sensed someone on the other side—probably the partner of the guard she'd knocked out earlier.

Violently, she kicked open the door. The man leaped back and pulled some small daggers from his vest. His reflexes were as quick as she would have expected from someone of his ilk. But the blades he threw didn't hit home; they bounced off the mysterious barrier and stuck fast into the walls on either side.

"Hey—"

As he attempted to shout out, Cecilia used her sweeper to deliver an uppercut to the man's chin. His jaw quivered as he passed out.

"That would've been close without the Artifact..." She sighed, taking a breath. She tied him up, gagged him, and threw him down the stairs before locking the door.

Now no one should find her out for a while.

Everything's gone pretty well, but I'm not gonna be able to make a clean getaway if I don't know where I am.

All she could make out through the window were trees. The architecture of the building made it clear that this was an ancient castle, but she had no idea where it was located.

Wish I had a map, but the next best thing would be a proper weapon.

The sweeper had broken. That one strike was as far as it could go.

Although no one could injure her, she still had to stay completely vigilant. Her Artifact might have some sort of weakness she wasn't aware of. And besides, its specialty was defense. If she wound up surrounded, she'd get captured without a doubt.

I'll start by heading to the armory and looking for a weapon I can use.

Checking that the coast was clear in all directions, she rushed out into the corridor.

"Gilbert, wait!" called Mordred, reining him in as he tried to run off. Behind him were Oscar and Jade, as well as Lean, who looked guilty and miserable. She'd just run to the boys' dorm for help and had told them that Cecil was abducted.

Eyeing Gilbert as he attempted to leave, Mordred insisted calmly, "You are the legitimate heir to House Sylvie. I cannot sanction any rash courses of action. While I do understand that you and Cecil are close, you must leave this to the proper channels of authority."

He went on, addressing Gilbert's back. "Additionally, Cecil is a baron's son. Risking your life for him is unseemly in the first place. Surely, you understand the value of your life. As the prospective successor to the prime minister, you can't follow your whims alone."

Gilbert was the genuine heir to House Sylvie, the highest-ranked family in the nobility. On top of that, he'd been endorsed as the next prime minister, hence why Mordred had reminded him he shouldn't put his life on the line for a noble of lower standing. He knew that.

It made perfect sense. All straight facts.

In aristocratic society, rank determined the value of someone's life, despite the fact that they were all equally human.

Instead of nodding, Gilbert whipped around. "I'm going to save Cecil, no matter what anyone says. Feel free to try and stop me, but I doubt you'll be able to."

"Do you know where he is?"

"I have a lead."

That would be Dante. Gilbert knew that his event was happening right now. In other words, he only needed to wring that information out of Dante, even if it meant getting a little rough with him. That was Gilbert's plan.

He turned to go, as if to say the conversation was over.

"Gilbert!"

"Gilbert," Oscar cried, his voice overlapping with Mordred's. He blocked Gilbert's path, his expression grim.

"...Your Highness."

"Dr. Mordred is right. At this rate, your parents are going to end up receiving unpleasant news. When people at the top give special attention to a lower-ranked noble, it complicates things down the line. You need to calm down for the time being."

"How am I supposed to be cool and collected right now?! I'm sure you don't know this, but Cecil is my s—"

If he revealed that Cecil was his foster sister Cecilia, they would all be forced to respond. Cecilia was a duke's daughter and the crown prince's fiancée. She far outranked her peers.

Gilbert knew that revealing her identity was the safest, most surefire method to getting what he wanted. But it would be tantamount to undoing the entire foundation she'd laid.

When he thought of her reaction after their reunion, he couldn't quite find the words.

Intercepting Gilbert's moment of hesitation, Oscar ventured, "New soldiers started working at the palace this April."

"What does that have to do with—?"

"Oh, just you listen. Anyway, the palace has recently been floating around the idea of them practicing a surprise attack. They've planned a large-scale drill that will also involve veteran soldiers with two to three years' experience."

Catching Oscar's drift, Gilbert fell silent.

"So I was thinking of having that get underway now. What do you think?"

"...An astute judgment, Your Highness."

Their stilted, unnatural conversation left everyone else in the room astonished.

"However, the location for the practice maneuver has yet to be decided. Do you have any ideas about that? You did say you had a lead."

"I'll go look into that immediately."

"As a bit of a warm-up, I was planning on participating in the attack myself. What about you?"

"Yes, if I'm allowed to..."

"Got it. I'll send a letter to your parents and to the palace informing them of that, then. The series of events that are about to transpire are all part of a practice maneuver, and I will be responsible for everything."

Gilbert inclined his head.

Mordred interjected, his tone betraying exasperated disbelief. "That was quite the little skit you two just put on... But if you're going to go to such lengths, well, I won't stop you. Do as you please. I'll file the overnight stay permission slips."

"Thank you," Gilbert answered with a bow.

Lean, who'd been silent the entire time, suddenly chimed in. "May I also attend this practice maneuver?"

"Lean?!" yelped Jade from next to her. It was clear he would have never expected that from her.

"It's all my fault that this happened, so I want to do something to make up for it. I also know where Lord Cecil has been taken," she declared confidently.

Oscar shook his head. "Sorry, but I don't want to take any impediments along. Are you saying you won't tell us where Cecil's been taken unless we bring you with us?"

"All right, then. In that case...," Lean replied, then turned to Jade. She held out a hand. "Jade, give me your Sacred Artifact."

"Huh?"

"I mean, you didn't plan on giving it to anyone else anyway, so it's fine, right? Won't it be better to have multiple people who can camouflage themselves?"

"I guess...," he answered, shocked by her erratic request. But since it was coming from a friend, he handed over his bracelet to her.

"I don't want to become the Holy Maiden or anything, so I wasn't planning on collecting these," Lean noted as she slipped Jade's Artifact onto her right wrist. The ordinary silver bangle glowed faintly. "I just have to save him. I can't let him get killed because of me again."

Her eyes burned with a determination and intent that hadn't been there before. She waved the bracelet in Oscar's face. "Now I won't be an impediment to you, Prince Oscar."

"True enough... Do your best to keep yourself safe on your own."

"I understand."

The four of them, Jade included, then launched into a strategy meeting.

As he observed their discussion, Mordred spoke to himself, as if it had nothing to do with him. "The future king and the future prime minister. The son of a firm that controls the country from the shadows and the future Holy Maiden apparent… Just how important is this Cecil Admina?"

Right as those four were talking strategy, Cecilia was making her way down the corridor. She passed by a few people occasionally, but to her surprise, she was avoiding any and all attention by keeping quiet and walking purposefully. The organization must have been so massive that interpersonal connections didn't run very deep.

Armory, armory…

She wound her way along, subtly checking left and right.

That looks like it.

In the deepest part of the first floor of the old castle lurked a room—though it was more like a storehouse. It was the only place where the decorations had been noticeably pared down.

She edged closer apprehensively but found it unlocked. She slipped inside and lit a hanging lantern, illuminating the interior.

"Bingo!"

The chamber was filled with weapons. Innumerable swords hung on the wall with an equal number of shields below. Daggers, crossbows, and other small firearms were also in abundance.

The armor, helmets, cannons, and artillery didn't have an assassin vibe, so they must have been remnants from when the building was a true castle. So expansive was the oblong room that she couldn't see all the way to its end.

The farthest section of the chamber appeared to be unused. Toward the front stood a row of armaments that looked easy to carry. Cecilia picked out a dagger.

"I haven't used a real one much. I wonder if I'll be okay."

In her lessons, she'd always used fake swords made of metal. While the dagger's size and weight felt close to what she was comfortable with, using it in real combat would probably feel strange. Of course, that didn't mean she was going to settle for a fake sword...

Just as she belted the knife in its scabbard to her waist, the door suddenly opened behind her to reveal a familiar face.

With no opportunity to hide, Cecilia came face-to-face with the intruder.

"It's you..."

In stepped Marlin, living up to her position as the leader. Her eyes grew wide when she realized it was Cecilia; perhaps she'd memorized all her subordinates' features.

Cecilia instantly took a huge step back. She had no idea what to do. When she started by creeping her hand down to the blade she'd just equipped herself with, Marlin shut the door behind her without calling for anyone else.

Stunned, she noted, "I didn't expect you to break yourself out of our dungeon."

Although Cecilia remained wary of Marlin's lack of hostility, she removed her hand from the dagger.

"I thought you'd be a bit more refined since you're a young lady of nobility," Marlin commented, sitting atop an empty box nearby.

"Um...so you're not going to capture me?" Cecilia replied, voicing the question in her heart.

"What good would that do? I was originally planning to let you go tomorrow morning anyway."

"What?"

"How would it benefit me to tick off the duke and his clan? I still prize my life, you know," Marlin remarked carelessly, jiggling her legs.

"But earlier..."

"That was just some posturing. This group's gotten kinda big, and I've got a lot of annoying guys who love to prattle on about how they'll take revenge if they quit or that we need to get our coin by any means necessary. Now there are even a few here who wanna take it upon themselves to act like common bandits. I just had to grill the hell out of those three." Marlin sighed with a grimace, cracking her shoulders.

She was an entirely different person from the woman Cecilia had met before.

"It's not good to let the scope get so out of hand. At first, I was just trying to make a band of chivalrous assassins who only killed the bad guys. Now it's devolved into a bunch of cutthroats who'll kill anyone if they're paid to do it."

Keeping quiet, Cecilia listened to Marlin's monologue. While her hands weren't clean, she didn't seem like a bad person at her core.

"So when Dante defected, I thought that would be the perfect excuse to make some changes, since he was our biggest earner. If I care about his happiness, I shouldn't keep him tied to this place."

She looked like an older sister worrying about her baby brother—maybe that was their actual relationship. The game doesn't go into it in detail, but it *does* seem strange that someone of Dante's caliber would labor under another's heel for no reason.

"And just when I was going to take this chance to dissolve the organization, you showed up."

"Me?"

"Yep. My stupid leading members have been making noise for some time now about abducting an aristocrat to get ransom money. So they pulled that stunt just now, looking to get revenge on Dante at the same time. Though I bet it also was supposed to be some sort of rebellion against me, since I've always been opposed to the kidnapping business."

Apparently, Heimat wasn't a monolith. Marlin's story implied that there were people hostile to her in the organization.

She got off the empty box. As she brushed dust off the seat of her pants, she faced Cecilia. "Well, anyway. That was a long-winded way of saying that I meant to let you go from the start. I never thought you'd bust yourself out on your own. I actually just came to the armory to pick out a weapon to give you tomorrow, since I thought you'd have trouble if I sent you off on your merry way unarmed."

"I…see," Cecilia answered with a nervous nod. She didn't trust this woman completely, but Marlin had no reason to lie to her.

Marlin's gaze shifted to the dagger at Cecilia's waist. "But I guess if you've already made your choice, that's that… Follow me. Now's our chance. I'll send you back to your school."

"Oh, okay."

Leading the way, Marlin reached for the door. But…

"Hmm?"

"What's wrong?"

"The door won't open," Marlin answered, rattling the knob over and over again. While she was doing that, gray smoke slowly crept in from the crack under the door. Upon placing a hand to the wood, she felt the slightest bit of warmth.

"Damn. I screwed up," she cursed tensely. Cecilia broke into a cold sweat.

Biting her lip and looking cornered, Marlin turned to Cecilia and shouted at her, "Get out of the way!"

Cecilia stepped to the side as ordered. Then Marlin hurled herself against the entryway. With a loud crash, the door—hinges and all—fell outward.

"Looks like we've been set up."

Fire and smoke filled the corridor. Bright flames licked at the curtains and wood.

A cold chill ran down Cecilia's spine. "What's going on?!"

"A fire—one someone set on purpose. They must be trying to get rid of everyone they can't handle all at once."

"Which…means?"

Marlin pointlessly nodded and held Cecilia's nose shut. "They went with the flow of the situation and kidnapped you even though they aren't actually bold or prepared enough to defy the house of the duke. Now they've gotten cold feet. Abducting the duke's daughter is a serious crime, no two ways about it. The country will devote everything it has to shutting down the organization, so they're going to push all the blame onto me and kill us off together."

"What?!" Cecilia screeched.

"If I die here along with you, they can say it was all my fault. Plus, if it works, they can take over the whole group. Seems like something those idiots would cook up."

"Boss!" shouted a man who looked like one of her underlings from the other side of the flames. He wanted to come to their aid, but the blaze and smoke were blocking him.

Marlin pointed to the exit. "You guys escape first! I'll follow later!"

"But—"

"Go now!"

"…Okay! Stay safe!"

"You too!"

Marlin must have been a good boss. The men wore looks of regret as they passed by.

"All right, what do we do? They've set this fire to roast you and me to death. They've even set the weapons alight," said Marlin. Ordinarily so self-possessed, now even she sounded panicky.

The inferno had engulfed both the corridor before them and the stairway to the second floor. To make matters worse, the deepest part of the blaze was located near the windows, so escaping through them was also out of the question.

Going deeper into the armory would allow them to temporarily escape the flames, but then they'd be trapped. It would only delay their fate, at most.

"You okay? You're white as a sheet," Marlin noted. Cecilia realized for the first time that she was shaking like a leaf. She was scared about losing her life, of course, but she could sense that her terror originated from somewhere else.

Her teeth ground together as her whole body tensed up. She was so frightened that cold sweat beaded over almost every inch of her skin. Finally, she forced herself to nod. "I'm fine."

"You don't look it. Seems like we can still head that way, so let's go."

"Okay."

Marlin set off and Cecilia attempted to follow, but then there was a sickening *crunch* and a post above her head came crashing down.

"AHHH!"

It all happened too suddenly for her to move. Her entire body had frozen stiff.

It had been longer than thirty minutes since she'd touched the Artifact, so she couldn't expect any automatic defense from it.

Bracing for impact, she squeezed her eyes shut. Just then, someone sent her flying.

"Aaahhh!"

She plunged into the wall, her back colliding against it with such force she was briefly winded.

Cautiously, Cecilia opened her eyes, only to find Marlin squashed beneath the thick timber. The other woman had protected her.

"Are you okay?!" Cecilia cried, flying over in a panic. The beam lying on top of Marlin was heavy but not so heavy that someone couldn't manage to lift it up. Cecilia moved the pillar aside and placed a hand under Marlin's back, pulling her up. Her palm cradling the back of the other woman's head came away bloody. Noticing how Marlin couldn't move even if Cecilia supported her, she wondered if Marlin had broken bones somewhere.

"Why would you...?"

"Because you can't get hurt."

"Because I'm the daughter of a duke?" she blurted out, deliberating about why that should be the reason.

Marlin shook her head weakly. "There's that, too, of course. But I did it because you're Dante's friend. If you got hurt, he'd be furious with me."

"Friend?"

"I'm not sure why, but the last time he came back, he seemed overjoyed as he told stories about you. He mentioned that there was a very interesting girl who was dressing as a boy to go to school..."

Marlin laughed, adding that right after that, he'd announced he was leaving the organization.

"Cecilia, was it? Leave me here. I can't run anymore." She winced, her head lolling from side to side as she began to lose consciousness from blood loss.

Cecilia raised her voice, trying to keep her conscious. "I can't do that!"

"What do you think you're saying? I'm the head of the organization that abducted you."

"But you still saved me."

"Don't...waste your breath on that... Hurry..." Marlin wheezed before passing out in Cecilia's arms.

She looked all around her. "What do I do now...?"

The path they were about to take was now engulfed in flames.

For now, I've gotta think of something.

Cecilia hoisted Marlin onto her back. She was only safe now because of her; she couldn't leave her behind.

"Ngh!"

Pain shot through her right ankle as she took on Marlin's

weight. When she turned to examine it, she saw that it was swollen and red. She must have twisted it when she'd been thrust away earlier. But it was a light scratch compared to Marlin's condition.

She touched the Sacred Artifact again. The barrier went up, enveloping Marlin who was slung over her back as well.

"I'll go to the back of the armory for now..."

She knew doing that would only slow things down. But it was the only way to escape the fire. Gilbert's Artifact could only reflect physical blows—it could do little in the face of smoke and flame.

Cecilia hobbled to the rear of the armory on her sprained ankle. A small part of her had hoped there might be a window there. But...

"You've gotta be kidding me..."

There was indeed a window. It was inlaid with a square pane of decorative stained glass to let light in. Breaking that glass would turn it into a perfectly serviceable escape route.

"There's no way..."

But the opening was placed absurdly high on the wall. It was so far up that Cecilia couldn't have reached it even if she had two of herself.

And with her ankle twisted and Marlin on her back, it was hopelessly out of reach.

"No, no, no..."

Smoke started to permeate the space. Blood trickled down the shoulder that Marlin's head rested on. If she didn't receive treatment soon, she might die.

"CECIL!"

Just as she heard that voice, the stained-glass window shattered before her eyes. Then someone plunged down in a natural fall.

"Wha—? Dante?!"

There stood Dante, rope in hand. He wore a determined expression, his usually flippant grin hidden below the surface. Noticing

Cecilia, he dashed over. "Are you okay?! I heard our guys had done something stupid and came running!"

"Uh, yeah. I'm fine, but…"

Dante's gaze moved from Cecilia to the woman slumped over her back. The sight obviously rattled him. To Dante, Marlin was like a mother, father, and older sister all in one. Seeing her bleeding and unconscious had to be unnerving.

After going very still for several seconds, he immediately turned back to Cecilia. "Cecil, we're going to bust out of here."

"Okay."

"So first, leave Marlin."

"What?"

"I can only carry up one person at a time."

His words turned her insides to jelly. He looked completely serious, not joking in the slightest.

"Cecil, you can't climb up the rope with your ankle, can you? I can carry one person but not two."

"But—"

"Unlike you, Marlin brought this on herself." He sighed, sadness and regret evident in his gaze. He evidently longed to save Marlin, too.

The flames had almost reached them. If he took Cecil up first, Marlin's body might be set alight by the time he came back down. Dante had decided to let her die.

"Isn't Marlin important to you, Dante?"

"People like us don't get to die peacefully anyway."

"But still—"

"Hurry! The blaze is coming this way," he snapped, cutting her off. He pulled her close to him, but Cecilia shook his hand away.

No! I refuse!

"Cecil!" he gasped reproachfully.

She bit her lower lip. Life was precious. That was why Cecilia had begun working away at her scheme ever since she'd learned of her own fate. While it wasn't as though she'd toiled endlessly, Cecilia had spent twelve years doing everything in her power to avert her demise.

It was all for a chance to live out the rest of her days without a care in the world.

But Cecilia didn't intend to save her own life at the expense of someone else's. If she was destined to succumb, then leaving Marlin to die instead meant foisting Cecilia's fate onto the other woman.

And that was the one thing she absolutely could not do.

And besides...

She could understand why Dante adored Marlin so much. She was his one and only family in the world. If he made the call to let her die, he would bear that weight for the rest of his life.

Cecilia summoned a smile to her face. "Dante, take Marlin up first."

"But—"

"I have this, so I'll be all right," she lied, showing him her Sacred Artifact. "With this one activated, no attacks can harm me. That goes for fire and smoke, too."

She'd mixed some lies into the truth. Not for nothing, she was a former theater kid; Dante shouldn't have suspected a thing. "If you get me out of here first, you'll never be able to save her. But if you rescue her first, then you can save both of us."

She took his hand. "I'm fine, so please help Marlin first! I'll use this to keep myself safe while waiting for you to get back."

"Really?"

"Want to punch me to try it out? But it's got a pretty nasty recoil, so it might do more than just hurt."

After some consideration, Dante finally gave a slow nod. "All right. Once I've brought Marlin out, I'll come right back to rescue you."

"Okay. I'll be waiting right here."

Dante transferred Marlin from Cecilia's back to his. Then he scrambled nimbly up the rope. Cecilia leaned against the wall, watching until they went out of sight.

"I really put on a performance just now..."

She had no regrets. But she was definitely scared.

Would Dante make it back in time? In her estimation, he probably wouldn't. She couldn't count on aid arriving from any other avenue, either. Even if someone showed up, they wouldn't expect her to be trapped in the middle of a blazing armory.

Had she given up? No, but at the moment she couldn't do a thing.

Upon closing her eyes, she beheld a confusing scene that seemed both familiar and alien.

A movie theater on fire.

In front of her she saw her best friend, the one she'd meant to rescue, collapsed next to the woman her friend had attempted to save.

Her sleeve then caught fire...

"Aaaahhh!" she shrieked, batting at her sleeve in the real world without thinking. That one wasn't burning yet, of course.

After a moment of bewilderment and confusion, she wrapped her arms around herself to calm down.

"Oh, so I died in a fire..."

The fire had paralyzed her with horror because it had activated memories from her past life, stoking unconscious fear. That was also why she was trembling too much to move right now.

At last, the inferno began to spread inside the armory.

She shook with fear. Her knees stopped obeying her; she could hardly stay upright.

This may very well have been her fate. She was destined to die amid the flames.

Even though Gil and Oscar finally started getting along and everything...

Smoke clogged the air as a harbinger of the blaze to come. She began to feel faint and crumpled to the floor.

"I wanted to *live* this time…," she managed to say before losing consciousness.

"CECIL!"

"SISTER!"

By the time she heard those voices calling her, only a short amount of time had passed.

She opened her eyes to find an ashen-faced Gilbert peering in at her, the moonlight on his back.

"Gil…?"

"Are you okay?!"

I can see the moon, so that means I'm…outside…?

Sluggishly, she attempted to comprehend the situation.

She wasn't outside; she was still in the armory. But the wall that had just been there was now somehow rubble. It looked like a sword had sliced apart the wreckage on the ground.

"Gilbert, you carry Cecil! We're going to force our way out of here!"

She turned to see who'd shouted that. It was Oscar, his Sacred Artifact sword in hand while he faced in another direction.

Helpless, Cecilia let Gilbert pick her up.

"Cecil! Hang in there!" yelled Jade, running up beside them. They would be undetectable thanks to his Sacred Artifact's conceal abilities.

"Prince Oscar! There's fewer enemies this way!" a girl called out.

"Got it."

That exchange told her that Lean was here, too.

"You don't need to worry about a thing. Just sleep," Gilbert reassured her with a smile, very close to her.

For some reason, his voice soothed her anxiety so much that she wanted to cry.

Taking him at his word, she closed her eyes. Once she did, she slowly drifted off and lost consciousness but in a completely different context than she had before.

"Cecil, do you have anything to say to me?"

"I'm very sorry for running off on my own...," Cecilia apologized with her head bowed, propped up on a bed at the Vleugel Academy nurse's office.

A fearsome smile adorned Gilbert's features as he stood next to the bed imposingly, arms akimbo.

Dr. Mordred was absent from the office, having gone to the headmaster to discuss the circumstances. The room's current occupants were Cecilia, Gilbert, Oscar, and an unusually docile-looking Lean.

"Come on—don't get so upset with him. He's all right in the end, isn't he?" piped up Oscar from behind Gilbert, throwing Cecilia a lifeline.

Gilbert whirled to face him. "You're too soft on him, Your Highness! What Cecil deserves is a serious talking-to!"

"You're too agitated right now. When we went to go rescue him, you even got so carried away that you called Cecil 'Sister'..."

"Er, that was..." Gilbert trailed off, his face freezing as he stood petrified. It was unusual for him to mess up that way. He hadn't once slipped up like that before.

I know that just shows how worried he was about me..., she thought, feeling immensely guilty.

As she sat there with her head hung low, Oscar patted her head. "I suppose Gilbert does have a point, though. You can't put yourself in danger like that. I was scared to death."

"I know."

"You still haven't arranged for me to meet Cecilia. I can't have you going off and dying just yet."

"*Excuse* me?" snapped Gilbert.

Cecilia smiled at Oscar's jab, and it made his face soften, too. He reached out to stroke a self-reassuring finger down her cheek, and the warmth of it made her tense up a little. "Oscar?"

"Mmm. You're definitely alive."

"O-of course I am!"

"Raaaaaghhh!" Gilbert cried, splitting them apart by force. Then he marched right up to Oscar. "This is exactly what I'm talking about! This is why you're so shameless even though you're not trying to be!"

"What are you so wound up about?"

"What is going on inside your head for you to not be able to do it if you're aware of it but totally capable of it if you're not?!"

"Uh...I have no idea what you're saying, but I can tell you're insulting me."

They were back at it again. Cecilia lay back on the bed, a pained smile on her lips.

When she'd woken up in the nurse's office earlier, everything was already over.

Gilbert explained what had happened in the interim:

Immediately after the shadowy figures had abducted Cecilia, Gilbert and the others had rushed to go rescue her under the guise of a training exercise for new soldiers. By the time they'd arrived, however, the old castle was already on fire.

Leaving the fleeing Heimat assassins for the soldiers to take care of, the four students went to go save Cecilia but had no idea where she could be. That was when they ran into Dante, carrying a woman on his back. He told them where Cecilia was and what had happened in the armory. Dante himself had revealed his true identity to Oscar at that point.

Cecilia shot her eyes to the floor as it all came back to her. "Oh yeah, Oscar, about Dante...um..."

"Why do you look so concerned?"

"I mean, you know..."

In the game, discovering Dante's identity makes Oscar really depressed. She was worried because surely this Oscar must have been feeling the same way now, too.

But without taking her feelings into account, he responded bluntly, "I already knew."

"You what?"

"I knew everything about who Dante was from the beginning. I went along with his act because I already knew."

"What?!"

"Is something wrong with your brain, Your Highness? He was trying to kill you!" Gilbert burst out, unable to contain himself.

Oscar was nonplussed. "He admitted that he honestly wasn't up to it."

Arms folded, he really didn't seem like he'd been hurt at all.

How did it end up like this...?

The Oscar of the game is the definition of an aloof, solitary prince. He's calm, cool, and collected at all times but also consistently overbearing. He exudes an aura of hostility and shows no interest in anyone besides the heroine, Lean.

But the real Oscar—while he had his condescending moments—didn't boss people around at all. In fact, he was downright amicable.

The Oscar of the game would never associate with the likes of barons' sons at Cecil's station, but this one made friends with anyone, regardless of their social standing.

Maybe his dating sim counterpart doesn't care that much about Dante, either, Cecilia thought.

In contrast, this Oscar was interested in the people around him. Perhaps that was why he had noticed something odd about Dante at an early stage and had investigated it on his own.

As she was lost in thought, someone knocked shyly on the door to the nurse's office. When Cecilia called for them to enter, Jade poked his head in. "Oh, Cecil! You're awake."

"Mm-hmm. Sorry for worrying you."

"Oh no. I was just along for the ride. You should thank the two who did the real work, yeah?" he said. Then he seemed to remember something and looked over at Gilbert and Oscar. "Oh, right. Your Highness and Gil, some higher-ups want to speak to you. Apparently, they want a report on tonight's training exercise."

"Got it," noted Oscar.

"I'll be right there," added Gilbert.

They headed for the door and then turned back to look at Cecilia, who was watching them go.

"*Please* don't do anything unreasonable."

"I'll come back to check on you later."

"Bye!"

The three men all left parting words in their own particular styles before exiting the room. Now it was just Lean and Cecilia.

Uncharacteristically silent, Lean was curled up in a corner; she must have felt responsible for Cecilia's kidnapping.

"Lean? You okay? Are you hurt anywhere?" Cecilia asked, and Lean looked up. Her clear eyes bore right into Cecilia.

What is it? Is there something on my—? Oh, crap!

Suddenly recalling that she'd blown her cover in front of Lean, Cecilia broke into a cold sweat. Everyone else had reacted to her the same as usual, so she'd forgotten until just now.

Ugh, what can I do now? Is she going to investigate me now?

If she did, that on its own would be fine. Once everyone discovered her identity, Cecilia would return to her life as a doomed villainess. No, now that she'd deceived everyone on top of everything else, her fate might become even more dire than in the game.

"Uh, um…"

"So Lord Cecil was actually Lady Cecilia...," she remarked in a dark, foreboding tone.

Cecilia's entire body went taut as a wire. She gulped, certain that it was all over now. She'd been a fool for believing she could simply prance back to her old life.

"Lord Cecil. You...pff...decei— Pff, ah-ha-ha..."

"Huh? Lean...?" Cecilia started, staring at the other girl, who was acting even more strangely than usual. Lean tilted her head down and started to rock back and forth.

Almost as if she were laughing...

"Ha-ha-ha, I can't! Hiyono, you're too good!" Lean cried, bursting out into laughter. She was doubled over, giggling uncontrollably.

"What?! Lean, are you okay? Did something happen when you got kidnapped? Hit your head, perhaps?"

"Nope, I'm completely fine! Thanks to you protecting me, Hiyono."

"Nuh-uh, don't say I protected you when I just got caught in the end. That was pathetic."

"I beg to differ. Back then, Hiyono... You were so cool and brave that it gave me chills!"

"What? Really? You'd go that far to praise... Hmm?" Cecilia trailed off, blinking as she finally hit on what felt off about this.

Wait, huh? Lean just called me Hiyono...

As all the blood drained from her face, she turned over toward Lean only to find her grinning with amusement. Her expression did indeed feel familiar, but not thanks to anyone she'd met in this life. It was something she remembered from her past one.

Cecilia held up a hand. "Um, hold on a second. I'm trying to make sense of things in my mind right now..."

"Hiyono, not in my wildest dreams would I have expected you to transmigrate into Cecilia or that you'd be dressing as a boy! I'm cracking up—it's hilarious!"

"I said to hold on!" she shouted. But Lean didn't flinch at all and just kept guffawing. She was certainly in a good mood.

Her friend held up a finger. "Now I have a little quiz for you. Who was I in my past life?"

"You'd have to be Ichika, of course!"

"Ah-ha-ha! Yup, you got it!" Lean giggled, making a peace sign with both hands. That silly part of her hadn't changed at all.

"Unbelievable...," Cecilia whispered in a small, terse voice. Across time, space, and multiple universes, she had reunited with her best friend.

Epilogue

How did it even turn out this way...?

Several days after the kidnapping incident, Cecilia heaved a sigh as she made her way down a hallway. The students she passed by stared at her with curiosity, both boys and girls alike. The girls blushed, while the boys' gazes were filled with both awe and jealousy.

And it was no wonder, because word on the street was that Cecil had somehow managed to shut down Heimat solo.

In reality, Marlin had survived and simply dissolved the organization, but there were some reasons why that couldn't be the official story. Evidently, the nation's top officials preferred to have the organization "shut down" rather than "dissolved."

In that case, it should have been fine to say that it got shut down during the soldiers' training maneuver, but putting it like that would just open up a different can of worms. The training maneuver was just practice—a drill. Announcing that the authorities had chosen to train the soldiers using an actual combat scenario would be a real problem.

With so many different, conflicting opinions in the mix, the version of events where Cecil resolved the situation alone was ultimately deemed the least offensive.

In Cecilia's opinion, it was even *more* far-fetched that a single person could have driven an organization of assassins to destruction without any assistance. And yet, the official story basically went that Cecil used his knightly powers, then things proceeded well, then it all wrapped up nicely.

A masterfully opportunistic tale if she'd ever heard one. It might have been worse than something a kindergartner would write.

"But I didn't actually do anything...," she murmured to herself.

"You did save Marlin, though, which led to Heimat's shutdown. Isn't that close enough?" ventured Dante, who had appeared out of nowhere and started walking alongside her.

She jumped. "Don't creep up on me like that!"

"Ah-ha-ha. Sorry, sorry." Dante grinned, cheeky as usual. Any trace of the seriousness he'd showed when he'd come to rescue her had long since disappeared. Now he was just a cheerful, mischievous classmate.

"What happened to the Heimat people in the end? I heard some of them got captured as part of the practice maneuver."

"Ah, yeah. Those were all the ones who betrayed Marlin. She still has the original members with her 'cause they're all close."

Marlin had originally created Heimat as an organization that would bring people without family together and give them work to do. At first, the group was contracted to work as guards. But over time, as Heimat got offers to do other types of jobs, it turned into an association of assassins who eliminated people who made others suffer, like slave traffickers and black-market dealers.

Thus, the original crew from Heimat's early days were now more like family than coworkers.

"Anyway, are you sure you're okay turning down Marlin's offer?"

"Ah, that would kind of be too much responsibility for me..."

Marlin had started up another organization after dissolving Heimat. But it would be more accurate to say that she'd formed a spy group composed of an elite few—the original Heimat members. And she'd asked Cecilia if she wanted to be the new band's very first head.

A dozen or so members in the spy group—with Cecilia at the helm.

Instead of a duke's daughter, she would become more like a queen or even some sort of evil empress controlling the world behind the scenes.

Moreover, the members' skills were all tried and tested.

Ordinarily, she would have jumped at the opportunity, but she'd politely turned Marlin down, citing the danger of the project. All she wanted to do was live out a carefree, relaxing life. Marlin had been adamant for a while but ultimately accepted her answer.

"But you can just think of it as a slightly large-scale bodyguard association!" Dante said.

"Yeah, *too* large-scale," Cecilia instantly quipped. She wasn't ready to be an evil empress yet.

He pouted in dissatisfaction. "Hmph. Well, she's the type to repay a favor no matter what, so she'll put you first if you ever need anything in the future. Great, huh?"

"Ha-ha-ha...," she laughed dryly. No matter what anyone said, she didn't need such larger-than-life bodyguards.

Should the worst happen and the Killer shows up, I may just have her return the favor, though...

But she had a feeling that wouldn't be necessary.

Because it just feels like I'll be able to figure something out with everyone's help.

While that may have been overly optimistic, it was what Cecilia really believed. She would only call on Marlin's organization if she were *truly* in a bind.

Cecilia and Dante walked along and into the dining hall together. Lean leaped from her seat and waved at them. "Lord Cecil! Lord Dante!"

Surrounding her were Gilbert, Oscar, Jade, and Huey—who had recently been promoted to the title of Lean's boyfriend. They'd all made plans to study for exams together.

Cecilia sat down next to Lean, then whispered in her ear, "You're going to keep calling me that?"

"Yeah! It has a nice ring, doesn't it?"

"What ring...?"

Because Lean knew Cecilia's true personality, this only made her feel uncomfortable. And even though her friend was aware of Cecil's hidden identity now, she was still writing stories featuring a character based on Cecil—as the top, of course.

According to Lean, this was because *"I like it when a guy who's so pretty you'd think he's the bottom comes on strong and dominates the other guy."*

Cecilia still found her logic utterly incomprehensible, just as she had in their previous life.

Gilbert smiled as he opened up a notebook. "Summer break is coming up once exams are over. Study hard, Cecil."

"I—I will!"

"You guys are going back home, right? Be sure to let me see Cecilia during summer break."

"What?! Oscar, you're going to come over to our house?!" Cecilia yelped.

"It's not your house. It's Cecilia's manor."

"R-right...," she stammered, cold sweat beading on her cheeks.

Oscar might have been a bit thickheaded, but he'd still definitely figure out who Cecil really was once he laid eyes on Cecilia.

"In that case, I'd like to come over, too!" cried Lean, shooting her hand up with a half smile on her lips. She was probably thinking there was no way she wouldn't get a front-row seat to *that.*

"If Oscar's going, I wanna go!" cried Dante.

"Well, if Lean is going, then...," added Huey.

"I've always wanted to visit a duke's manor once in my life," chimed in Jade.

Cecilia paled. Her plans to relax over a nice summer vacation were disappearing fast. She racked her brain for a way to stop this from happening.

But aside from Cecilia and Gilbert, everyone else was excited about the idea of visiting Cecilia's manor. It was too late now.

"My summer vacation...," she whined to herself.

"Well, before that, you've gotta step up your studying, Cecil," Gilbert reminded.

"Huh?" she said, looking up at him.

"Aside from question number four there, all your answers are wrong."

"What?! Really?"

"Really."

For the moment, she had to save thinking about summer vacation until it was summer vacation.

She used the base of a pen to scratch her cheek.

A wild summer break was just around the corner, bringing with it a world of trouble.

✦ EXTRA ✦ The Melancholy of Gilbert

This is a tale that takes place five years before the start of our story…

There are several people I hate.

Specifically, my parents and brothers, who haven't once made an effort to see me since I came to live with the Sylvies. El, the gardener who obviously has a thing for my sister. I also can't stand Hans, the soldier who teaches her swordsmanship, and Donny, who for whatever reason has gained her trust the most.

I also despise all the aristocrats here at this royal gala who are trying to curry the favor of an eleven-year-old kid to get into House Sylvie's good graces. And I hate the girls who take my smile as permission to loop their arms through mine.

Out of all of them, though, the one I hate the very most is…

"Ah, Gilbert. You're here, too."

"Your Highness."

Oscar Abel Prosper.

Our crown prince and my sister's fiancé. He's the one I most detest.

He makes a beeline for me, a friendly smile on his lips. It feels like it's been a long time since he became the embodiment of the words *hard-headed* and *overbearing.*

"It's been about three months since we met at the garden party in the spring. So? How are you keeping?"

"Very well, thank you. You seem well also, Your Highness."

"Eh, can't complain."

I hate the way he can look down on me since he's a head taller. And he's grown a bit compared to last year, too. I'm going to hit my growth spurt someday… But I haven't caught up to him yet.

I plaster a formal smile across my face. "I have heard that the plan to suppress the revolt from the Meltt clan in the southeast was your idea, Your Highness."

"I only came up with the initial concept. Our military adviser, Marquis Girardan, developed it into a workable plan. I'm still much too inexperienced and don't have the power to stick my nose in politics."

"Still, Father praised the original plan. Called it ingenious, even."

"I'm quite glad to hear that. But I know you could have come up with a better one, Gilbert. The brilliance of the Sylvie heir has not only reached my ears—it has reached my father's as well."

"…Thank you."

I especially loathe the way he puts on this false modesty, even though he's extremely hardworking and accomplished. How easy it would have been for me to hate him if he were still the same overbearing tyrant prince he used to be.

If only my sister would just make something up and break off their engagement…

Life truly doesn't go the way you want it to.

The prince draws close to me and lowers his voice. "By the way, how's Cecilia?"

"…Fine."

"All right, then someday soon I'd like to…"

"You can't see her."

And here it is, the number one reason why I despise the prince.

He has a crush on my sister. What's more, he fell in love with her at first sight when he was six years old and has held on to those feelings ever since.

I'm aware how this sounds coming from me, but he's too persistent. I wish he'd just give up on her already…

"Can't you just let me see her already?"

"It is not for me to decide. Her health is too poor for her to meet with you."

"But you just said she's doing fine…"

"As I have just explained, it comes down to her being well enough to meet with you." I shut him down flatly.

He frowns and lets out a frustrated groan. "So wouldn't that mean she's *not* doing fine?"

"She is able to go about her life."

"So then…"

"Apparently, seeing you drains her energy and stamina," I say, purposely making it sound like hearsay, so it gives off the impression that my sister doesn't want to see him.

But he still won't give in. After a pause, he responds, "Tell Cecilia that she doesn't have to worry so much about my visit."

"Aren't you aware that your position makes that request impossible?"

"She and I will be husband and wife someday. She doesn't need to—"

"Currently, you are nothing more than strangers," I interrupt, the lowness of my voice surprising even myself. I have absolutely no intention of allowing them to marry. I'll do everything in my power to nullify the engagement.

He gives up on being so stubborn. Now he must get that it's pointless to ask me any further.

"I understand that I can't see her. In that case, could I ask you to give her my usual get-well gift? I tried to pick out something that a girl her age would like."

"All right…"

I can't very well reject a gift the crown prince personally selected, so once the party is over, I take it back to the manor and go to my sister's room.

There, she is lying in bed, having feigned illness. "Gil, you're back!"

"I am," I say, my heart warming at the ear-to-ear smile she offers to welcome me home. Already, I can no longer recall the melancholic feelings I'd been mired in. I give her the box that the prince passed to me.

"This is a gift from a noble who was concerned that you were absent from the party."

That wasn't a lie. The royal family technically counts as nobles.

"Ooh! Is it from the same person as always? Yay!" she enthuses, which puts me out of sorts.

She always reacts like this when I give her presents from the prince.

"This person and I have a lot in common!" She beams, her cheeks pink as she undoes the wrapping.

This is another thing I hate about him. He hasn't seen her in years, but every time, he's able to find her gifts she adores. And yet again…

"Wow! This chiffon cake looks delicious! Gil, thank the person who gave me this on my behalf!"

As ever, his present hits its mark.

She gazes at the chiffon cake in rapture, then tugs on my sleeve. "Hey, Gil."

"What?"

"Do you want to eat this whole cake together tonight without telling Mother and Father? I bet a top-secret midnight tea party would be really fun!"

She grins at me mischievously, and I find myself nodding. I indulge her like this every time; I've never refused her once. But I also still have my pride.

"You'll get fat, you know?" I say, slipping in a snide remark.

At that, her cheeks puff up in anger. "Then we'll split a slice!"

"You say that now, but I've seen this before. You always end up eating almost all of it in the end."

"So mean! That's because you're the one who feeds it to me!"

"Because you stare at me eating with such a greedy, hungry look that I'm forced to give in."

"Urgh…"

She's pouting, so I've probably been too mean to her. Before long, she'll end up in a full-blown sulk.

I take the cake box from her and stand up.

"Gil?" she asks, looking up at me.

I smile at her. "You wanted a slice, right? I'll go get one cut, so just wait here. Do you want your usual flavor of tea?"

"Yeah! Thank you!" she cries, nodding so happily that I'm entirely helpless before her. This has happened so many times before that I've become unable to refuse a single one of her requests.

I leave her room, cake box in hand. My steps are light as I make my way to the kitchen.

I hate the prince.

But just for today, I'm the tiniest bit grateful to him.

It will be another five years before that fateful day…

Afterword

First, I'd like to express my gratitude to each and every person who purchased this book. Thank you very, very much for buying *Cross-Dressing Villainess Cecilia Sylvie*! If you laughed even a little, noticed your heart beating faster, or felt excited while reading this novel, then there's no greater happiness for me! Additionally, I'd like to offer my heartfelt thanks to everyone at the publisher, and my editor Y, who all worked hard to bring this title to print! Thank you so much!

I was working on the serialization of this volume right in the middle of Golden Week. Every year, I spend Golden Week on vacation with my family, so it occurred to me that it would be entertaining to write a story about the characters all going on a trip together. If there were hot springs, I could write some prank scenes in the baths, and Gil and Oscar could do some naked bonding (hee). Plus, I really do want to write about Lean and Cecilia having some girl time!

I hope I can write a fun story like that someday...

Anyway, until we meet again somewhere in the future, remember to enjoy yourself!

Hiroro Akizakura